Praise for Shannon Stacey's
Taming Eliza Jane

"Taming Eliza Jane is without a doubt the best book that I have read in a long time."

~ *Fallen Angel Reviews*

"Ms. Shannon Stacy has done an excellent job writing this masterpiece. I thoroughly enjoyed reading it and will look for other works by her in the future. I highly recommend this great historical to anyone who likes a myriad of characters doing so much that the script never got dull!"

~ *The Romance Studio*

"Ms. Stacey pens an endearing historical romance with quirky, but loveable characters."

~ *Once Upon A Romance*

Taming Eliza Jane

Shannon Stacey

A Samhain Publishing, Ltd. publication.

Samhain Publishing, Ltd.
512 Forest Lake Drive
Warner Robins, GA 31093
www.samhainpublishing.com

Taming Eliza Jane
Copyright © 2007 by Shannon Stacey
Print ISBN: 1-59998-719-8
Digital ISBN: 1-59998-508-X

Editing by Angela James
Cover by Scott Carpenter

First Samhain Publishing, Ltd. electronic publication: June 2007
First Samhain Publishing, Ltd. print publication: November 2007

Dedication

My mother gave me a love of books, a love of cowboys—everybody from Louis L'Amour's Sacketts to Janet Dailey's Calders managed to sneak out of her room while she wasn't looking—and a whole lot of love in general. A long time ago, when I was just a very little girl, we drove to Texas and that was the biggest thing I'd ever known. I had no concept of the size of a galaxy or the universe then, just that grand and huge adventure. And one day I said "Mommy, I love you more than a three day drive."

It's funny now, of course. Who loves being in a car for three straight days? But at the time, that was my way of stretching my little hands all the way from Massachusetts to Texas and saying, "I love you *this* much."

Mom, I still love you more than a three day drive, and this one's for you.

Chapter One

When Eliza Jane Carter stepped down from the stagecoach, every man, woman and child on the street stopped to stare.

It wasn't only her incredible height of almost six feet that drew their attention. It wasn't only the combination of coal-black hair, ice blue eyes and a fine porcelain complexion. It wasn't even her lush figure, clad in a long, black skirt and severe, unadorned white blouse.

It was all of those things combined with a piercing, go-to-hell look that seemed to bore into the very soul of the town. With her back ramrod straight and her chin held high, she looked around the main street of Gardiner, Texas, just one more dingy cow town like the dozens she had visited before.

Her gaze lit on a woman in a worn calico dress with five children in tow. There was a woman standing silently in the hot sun while her husband conversed with a group of men. And there was a woman, her belly swollen with child, with an infant about a year old on her hip and a toddler clinging to her skirt.

Eliza Jane took a deep breath and gripped the handle of her valise. The women of Gardiner, Texas were about to be set free, and Eliza Jane Carter would be their George Washington, their Abraham Lincoln. She was a one woman revolution.

"Perhaps we could travel on just a little further?" Edgar whined at her side, dragging her away from her majestic musings.

Eliza Jane looked down at Edgar Whittemore, the man who was a constant thorn in her side. He was short, stout and possessed of a nasally voice and spectacles that refused to stay perched in their proper place, both of which drove her quite mad. But even worse was the circumstance under which he'd become her traveling companion. The insufferable horse's hind quarters of an attorney whose job it was to oversee her trust fund would only allow her access to those funds for her campaign if she remained *chaperoned* by a man of his choosing—to protect her from her own foolish feminine folly, of course. And that man was Edgar Whittemore.

"This is where Mr. Millar is sending the money, Edgar, so this is where we shall stay." Arrangements were made in advance according to a predetermined schedule, a fact he well knew. Edgar simply never passed up an opportunity to grate on her nerves.

Her mind made up, Eliza Jane squared her shoulders and hefted her bag, knowing Edgar would meekly follow suit. The arid inferno that was Gardiner was already draining her of energy and she wanted to find the hotel and soak in a cool, scented tub.

She made her way up the plank sidewalk lining the main street, keeping close to the buildings for shelter from the sun and wind. Noise assaulted her from every direction. Jingling harnesses, creaking wagons and the shouts of working men were nearly drowned out by the hot wind scraping across the town. The buildings seemed to groan as shutters banged and signs slapped against clapboards. And the sand... She could already feel it sifting through her hair to her scalp.

It was a far cry from green and lush Philadelphia, but Eliza Jane considered herself a soldier in the war to better the lives of her fellow women, and she'd trod many a battlefield as filthy and noisy as this. It would take more than an inhospitable environment to sway her from her chosen path.

She was a soldier who chose her own battles, and she chose to fight them in towns such as Gardiner. While many women, as well as men sympathetic to the cause, fought valiantly for some semblance of equality in the world of men— voting, for example—Eliza Jane fought smaller skirmishes on the home front, urging women to fight for respect in their own worlds.

She believed women had a fundamental right to accept or refuse intimate relations with their husbands, to bear children or not. She believed a woman should control her own money, lest she be forced to give herself to another man merely for survival should she become widowed or cast aside.

Standing on makeshift stages, spewing rhetoric to the uneducated masses accomplished little, in her opinion. Rather than trying to change life for the many by giving speeches to the few, Eliza Jane traveled, trying to teach small groups of women to enact changes for themselves.

But her cause was not free of personal peril. Men naturally did not care for their lives being disrupted. When their wives—little more than domestic and sexual slaves—began demanding respect, their anger invariably turned on the catalyst for the change, Eliza Jane.

Still, she wouldn't give up the fight. Couldn't, really, because it was all she had. With no desire for another husband and no hope of children, the fight for women's rights not only gave her life purpose, but kept the days from yawning endlessly in front of her.

So she tolerated the staring, whether they were looks of curiosity or hostility. She tolerated Edgar's whining. It's why she tolerated sweat running down her back and sand in her scalp—maybe a few less women would suffer her fate.

Edgar cleared his throat, and she realized they had reached their destination. The Gardiner Hotel was a plain two-story building with a false front and a small, unadorned sign announcing itself.

A brass bell heralded their entrance, and the skinny, red-headed clerk behind the desk didn't hide his surprise well at all. Clearly very few people stayed voluntarily in Gardiner, Texas.

"Help you?" the clerk asked, fully meeting her expectations by addressing the question to Edgar.

"We will require two rooms," Eliza Jane responded, perhaps a trifle too loudly, as she stepped in front of her chaperone. "Our date of departure is as yet unknown, but I am awaiting a delivery. As the next stage will not arrive for ten days, that will be our minimum length of stay."

The clerk blinked, then dropped his gaze to the register. "Yes'm. I'll just need your names."

"I am Mrs. Eliza Jane Carter of Philadelphia, and my traveling companion is Mr. Edgar Whittemore, also of Philadelphia."

The clerk's Adam's apple bobbed as he swallowed nervously. "I see. I...uh..."

Eliza Jane raised a questioning eyebrow at the man. Usually she didn't encounter resistance until she began her work in the town. Checking into a hotel was rarely a stumbling block unless the clerk or the owner was particularly fanatic in his or her faith. "Is there a problem, Mr.—?"

"Uh...Dan. Would you be a widow, then, Mrs. Carter?"

She felt embarrassment staining her cheeks, but she only lifted her chin, hoping he would mistake the blush for righteous anger. "As I requested separate rooms for Mr. Whittemore and myself, I cannot see how my marital status is at all your concern."

How she wished she didn't abhor lying. It would be so easy to simply proclaim herself a widow and be about her business.

"My apologies." Dan's face was nearly as red as his hair, and she felt a pang of sympathy for the man. She knew she was intimidating—it was a persona she had perfected as well as a stage actress perfected the role of Desdemona. "I'll just go get your keys, ma'am."

Relief tempered the sense of humiliation. She despised telling people the insufferable Augustus Carter had divorced her. *Divorced!* Cast out like trash because she failed to bear him a child. He had publicly declared her a failure not only as a wife, but as a woman, and the shame burned just slightly stronger than the flames of her convictions.

And the horrible, odious Mr. Millar, who controlled her dead mother's money and therefore Eliza Jane's purse strings, knew it. He delighted in the appointment of Edgar as her chaperone rather than the customary matronly female precisely because it put her in these awkward situations.

Widowhood would smooth her way slightly, but dishonesty would only undermine her personal sense of integrity. With her dignity stripped away, integrity and her cause were all she had left from which to draw strength.

The irony of doing her work while under the boots of two men made her very nearly want to spit, but as long as she could change the lives of even a few women for the better, she would accept the legal strictures of a society slow to change.

But change *would* come. The war would be won in the small battlefields of small towns like this one. When she left Gardiner, it would be a better place and Eliza Jane would get on that stagecoach with her chin held high. And the women she left behind would hold their heads a little higher, as well.

෨෫෬ය

Women, in general, were more of a pain in the ass than a lumpy saddle. And whores, in particular, could drive a sober man to go looking for the bottom of a bottle.

The one between whose thighs Will Martinson currently knelt—a particular favorite of his by the name of Sadie—giggled again, causing her ample breasts to shake. It was more of a distraction than any man could withstand. But Sadie liked baring them, even though he'd told her time and time again he had no need to see them.

"It ain't supposed to tickle, Sadie."

"I ain't laughin' at no tickle. Was laughin' at your face—so serious and businesslike."

Will pushed to his feet and flipped Sadie's skirt down over her splayed thighs. "When were your last courses?"

The amusement drained from the pretty whore's face. "Do I gotta baby in me, Doc?"

Will sighed and closed up his bag. His monthly health checks at the Chicken Coop were usually uneventful. Miss Adele took good care of her girls, and taught them to care for themselves. But he was especially fond of Sadie—a dirt-poor Southern farm girl who'd probably never make it to California no matter how much time she spent on her back—and her expression damn near broke his heart.

"I think you do, Sadie." And not the first inkling of which of her numerous customers may have fathered it. Not that it mattered. A whore's bastard was a child only the mother would love.

"How long can I work?"

His fingers tightened on the straps of his medical bag. "You should get on the next stage and go home, sweetheart. I'll pay your passage if you don't have enough money tucked away. Tell your folks you had a husband but he got killed."

A look of revulsion passed over her face. He saw that look a lot if he mentioned *home* during his visits to the Coop. What horrors these girls had been born into that made it preferable to spread their legs for an endless stream of strange men, he couldn't even begin to guess.

"I asked you," Sadie insisted, some of the sweetness gone from her voice, "how long can I work?"

Looking down into her pretty hazel eyes, framed by a mass of golden curls, he almost offered to marry her. She'd make a right sweet wife and she could be a proper mother to her baby. And if the people of Gardiner took issue with their doctor marrying a whore, why they could deliver their own babies and set their own goddamn broken bones.

He took a deep breath and settled his hat on his head. But, *hellfire,* he couldn't save them all.

"I guess until the men ain't willing to pay for you anymore," he replied in a voice heavy with regret.

Will walked out of the Chicken Coop with an aching heart and a gut churning with frustration. The last person he expected to see waiting for him was the sheriff, who usually gave the only whorehouse in town a wide berth.

Adam Caldwell was damn near the best friend Will had ever had, but he could be as much a pain in the ass as the whores at times. He wasn't sure he had the patience for him right now.

The sheriff fell into step beside him on the plank sidewalk. Will knew they made a noticeable pair. Adam was dark and forbidding. Over six feet of sun-darkened muscle, black shirt and a black hat covering long black hair, with unforgiving eyes almost as dark. They all figured there was some Indian in him somewhere, but no man had yet had the balls to ask him outright.

Will himself was as tall, but he was leaner, with an open, friendly air about him. White shirt with cuffs rolled to the elbows tucked into denim pants. His battered, brown Stetson covered sandy hair he kept trimmed off his ears and neck. And the ladies sure did tend to go on about his blue eyes.

The only other things they had in common were the tin stars—Will liked to pin his on his doctoring kit—and the holsters low on their hips. Will Martinson had sworn to preserve life, but he was also the only man Adam trusted to back him up. The sheriff's reputation went a long way toward keeping the peace, but when there was need for a deputy, Will just told himself there was more than one way to preserve a life.

"Trouble?" Adam finally asked when Will didn't talk just to fill the silence as he was wont to do.

"Sadie's with child."

Adam shrugged. "Can't help those who don't wanna be helped, Doc."

Hell, he knew that. But he wasn't in the mood to hear it just yet. "Heard at the Coop some woman got off the stage and stayed off."

It was a rare event for a woman to stay in town, unless her intention was a room at the Chicken Coop. Word of her had spread through Gardiner like wildfire.

"Yup. Ain't good."

Will waited for his friend to go on with a growing sense of aggravation. *Hellfire*, he'd had easier conversations with mules. "Why ain't it good? She somebody you've heard of?"

"Yup. Eliza Jane Carter. Likes to ride into town, get the women all riled up about demanding their rights and shit, then she skedaddles."

"She stayin' a while?"

"Looks like."

Will knew his friend was mulling over the woman's unwelcome presence in his town and her potential for troublemaking, but all he could think about was how the woman could maybe talk some sense into Sadie. Tell her there were better ways for her and her child to make it in the world.

Adam sighed and pushed his hat back on his head. "If the women gettin' riled up gets the men riled up, we could have us some trouble."

Damnation. He didn't need spectacles to see where Adam was heading with this. "Dammit, Adam, I'm a doctor, not a nanny."

"Better job for you than me. I ain't so good with diplomacy."

"Diplomacy? You? Shit, they say you shot a man for calling your horse ugly."

The sheriff shrugged. "He lived. And my horse ain't ugly."

Fact was, Sheriff Caldwell's gelding was the ugliest son of a bitch to ever stand on four legs. A sane man would have shot the creature just to save his own eyesight. But that horse had speed and stamina the likes of which Will had never seen, and he would run until his heart exploded for Adam. He was loyal in a way Will hadn't come across even in a good dog, and certainly never in another person. Didn't change the fact the beast was damn ugly, though. Folks had just gotten real quiet about it.

"I ain't asking you to marry the woman, Doc. Just keep an eye on her." When Will hesitated, Adam shrugged again. Hell, he hated that—made Will want to shove the sheriff's head so far down his neck he could never shrug his shoulders again. "I'd hate for her to cause trouble. Seems a mighty shame to shoot a woman."

Will laughed at the blatant attempt at blackmail, some of the tension easing from his body. "Even you wouldn't shoot a woman, you ornery son of a bitch."

He looked up in time to see a damn fine looking woman step out of the hotel. She was tall and thin, but not so thin she didn't have rounded breasts and hips that like to make a man's mouth water. "Is that her?"

"Must be."

Will smiled and pushed his own hat back a little further on his head. "It *would* be a damn shame to have to shoot her."

"Yup."

She liked to get women all riled up about their rights, did she? "Could be she starts causing too much trouble I'll have to put her over my knee and spank some sense into her."

And damned if he didn't get so riled up himself he had to walk down the sidewalk with his bag held in front of his crotch like a schoolboy.

Chapter Two

Eliza Jane felt immeasurably refreshed after her scented bath. The effects wouldn't last long now that she was back on the street, but at least she'd washed the grime of the stagecoach ride away and she looked her best for her first foray into the town.

As far as she knew, Edgar was still in his room, but she'd been unwilling—after the confines of the stagecoach—to wait for him any longer. She needed to stretch her legs and get to know Gardiner.

As a rule, the social climate of a town determined how she got started. In some places she could give a lecture in an opera house or schoolroom. In others, she was forced to be more discreet, speaking to smaller groups of women in their parlors or anywhere else they could find.

Her attention was caught by two men walking down the sidewalk toward her. One was tall and dark, with a star pinned on his chest. The other was as tall, but fair, with a star pinned improbably to a medical bag. And there was not a doubt in her mind they were heading straight for her.

Her reputation preceded her, apparently. Occasionally in the past, she'd been approached by the local law enforcement and warned to keep her opinions to herself. She'd even been bodily placed inside of a stagecoach in one particularly rough town. It was an embarrassment she didn't care to repeat any time soon.

No, she didn't especially care for the law. Though she tried not to think about the time her asking them to intercede on behalf of an abused wife had led to disastrous and heartbreaking results, she was inherently distrustful of them when it came to her cause.

As the two men closed in, Eliza Jane very nearly regretted leaving Edgar behind. He wasn't physically threatening by any means, but men tended to speak to her in a more civil manner when he was close by.

"Howdy, ma'am," the one with the medical bag said, tipping the brim of his hat. The other man only glared at her.

"Good afternoon, gentlemen." Eliza Jane maintained the smile she'd long ago perfected—polite and friendly, but still determined. She might tremble on the inside, but she never let it show.

"My name is Will Martinson, but most folks around here just call me Doc. On account of my being the town doctor and all." The other man snorted, but otherwise remained silent. "This is Sheriff Adam Caldwell."

"I'm pleased to make your acquaintance," Eliza Jane replied, purposely not mentioning her name. It was something of a little test she used to see how much, if anything, strangers knew about her.

"Don't make trouble in my town, Mrs. Carter," The sheriff confirmed her suspicions. "I sure would hate to have to shoot you."

And then he walked away, leaving Eliza Jane staring after him with her mouth hanging open in a most unladylike manner. How dare he threaten to shoot her? And his companion had the nerve to find it amusing?

"I do hope, Doctor Martinson, that you are about to tell me Sheriff Caldwell merely suffers from an extreme lack of social skills, but is really rather harmless in fact."

"Either Doc or Will, ma'am." He looked her up and down in an appallingly familiar manner. "I do believe I'd prefer hearing you call me Will."

She'd barely summoned enough indignation to reply when he smiled, completely disarming her. Her heart stuttered and she felt her cheeks flush as if she was but a simpering girl. She straightened her spine and lifted her chin, sending a message to her traitorous senses. This kind of foolishness would be neither entertained nor tolerated.

"As to Sheriff Caldwell," he continued, "he *is* sorely lacking in what you call social skills, but I wouldn't go so far as to call him harmless. He does seem to enjoy shooting people."

"With no cause?"

"Cause for a bullet means different things to different people. Walk with me."

He took her elbow and spun her around so swiftly she didn't have a chance to demur. He tucked her arm under his and led her down the uneven planks. She tried not to notice the muscles of his arm or the warm, spicy scent of him. It was merely in her best interest to make an ally of at least one of the town's lawmen.

"How is it, Doctor...Will, that you are both a doctor *and* an officer of the law? Wearing a sidearm in the manner of a gunslinger seems at odds with the Hippocratic Oath."

"To be honest, I wouldn't wear the deputy star for any man but Adam. There have been occasions on which the two oaths have come at odds with one another, but shooting the bad to preserve the lives of the good is a compromise I can live with. I sleep at night. How did you come to travel around getting happily married women all fired up?"

Eliza Jane stiffened against him. It was tempting to jerk herself out of his grasp and return to the hotel, but she was reluctant to make a spectacle of herself so soon. And, as she'd previously decided, she may need the doctor's good favor if she should run afoul of the sheriff.

"Most men will consider their women to be happily married rather than admit to problems for which they may be at fault."

"I've ain't married, ma'am, so I can't rightly speak to that. But I asked you to walk with me for another purpose."

Asked wasn't an entirely accurate description of how they'd come to be walking together, but Eliza Jane let it pass. More than a few of the townspeople had waved greetings to the doctor, and it was good to be seen in his company. Perhaps she would find her way somewhat smoothed socially.

"What purpose would that be?"

"Given Adam's bent toward shooting people, he asked me to be the one to watch over you and keep you out of trouble."

Eliza Jane's cheeks burned. "I already have a chaperone of sorts, if you will. My traveling companion, Mr. Whittemore—"

"Is probably as pussy-whipped as you want all men to be."

Eliza Jane stopped walking and tried to pull her arm away. "Doctor Martinson, I must object to the use of such language in my company!"

He didn't release her. "So you only want to be treated like a man when it suits you?"

"I assure you, Doctor Martinson, I do *not* want to be treated like a man. I simply want women to be afforded more respect than a man gives a horse."

"You'll find you'll get as much respect as you earn for yourself around these parts, Eliza Jane."

She didn't bother to call him on his overly familiar use of her given name. And when he nudged, she started walking again. There was no sense in arguing with him. Men were naturally the most resistant to her beliefs.

"Anyway," he said, "I figure I'll give you a little more freedom to do your preaching if you do a little favor for me."

"I do not preach. And what favor could you possibly need from me?"

"There's a whore that got herself in a family way. Her name is Sadie."

"Doctor, while I am able to educate women in ways to minimize the possibility of pregnancy, there is nothing I can—or *will*—do about it after the fact."

There were, in fact, ways in which women tried to end pregnancies, but Eliza Jane refused to be a part of such activities. Morality aside, the health risks were simply not to be ignored. Will Martinson, if he was any kind of doctor, should know that.

"You're a prickly thing, aren't you?" he asked in a cheerful tone that set her teeth on edge. They were nearing the end of the sidewalk and she wondered if they would turn around, cross the dusty street, or simply part ways. "I'd be real appreciative if you'd just talk to her. She doesn't know any life but whorin', and I thought maybe you could talk to her about how else a woman alone could raise up a child."

In today's society, her best option was to move to a new town, proclaim herself a tragic widow, and find herself a husband willing to raise another man's child. A man could populate an entire state with his bastards, but a whore and her illegitimate baby? It was a bleak future mother and child faced.

"Unless you're too good to talk to a whore," the doctor said tersely when she didn't reply right away.

"I don't turn away any woman in need, Doctor Martinson. I will gladly speak with Sadie, though I don't know how much help I can be. It will be very difficult to persuade a woman with an uncertain future to turn her back on a profession which provides her with income."

He had relaxed as she spoke, and his forearm brushed her ribs. Her body reacted to him like a thirsty man yearning toward a glass of water. Her pulse quickened, her breasts tingled, and she prayed the flush creeping up her neck didn't appear as feverish as it felt.

How utterly mortifying it would be to be caught lusting after a man she barely knew because of the slightest contact.

"But you're willing to talk to her?" he asked, apparently oblivious to her unseemly arousal. "I don't reckon you'd want to visit the Chicken Coop, so I can tell her a time to meet you somewhere else. My office, maybe, if that suits."

"Your concern for her future seems at odds, sir, with the fact you have so little regard for her situation you would have us meet in a chicken coop!"

The doctor stopped walking and laughed. He laughed so hard, in fact, that many a person paused to watch him. Eliza Jane, her arm finally freed, placed her hands on her hips. She certainly didn't find their conversation humorous in the least.

She'd resorted to crossing her arms and tapping her foot before Will managed to compose himself. Of course, it had taken all of her considerable self-control to keep from smiling herself. His laughter was probably the most infectious she'd ever heard.

"We passed the Chicken Coop during our walk, darlin'. See that pretty building with the flower pots in front?"

Eliza Jane stifled the small thrill she felt at hearing him drawl out that word *darlin'* and nodded. She'd noted in passing how pretty the flowers looked in this stark town and wondered at the work the building's residents must put into their care.

"That's the Chicken Coop. Gardiner's grandest—and only—house of ill-repute."

"Oh, I...they do grow beautiful flowers."

"Among other things," he added, and had the audacity to wink at her.

"You, sir, are incorrigible."

"Yes, ma'am."

Eliza Jane couldn't think of anything else to say. He was entirely too forward, but she dared not call him on it lest he remind her yet again he was simply treating her as he would a man. Not that he would be flirtatious with another man, of course, but in his general lack of manners.

She realized they were attracting some attention standing at the end of the sidewalk as they were. "Thank you for the walk, Doctor Martinson. I will send a note to Sadie at the first opportunity requesting a moment of her time."

"It's Will, and she can't read."

Eliza Jane sighed. The lack of educational opportunities for poor women sorely vexed her. "Then I shall visit her at the Chicken Coop. I assume mid-morning would be a...*safe* time to call upon her?"

"I'll tell her to expect you soon." He tipped his hat and grinned. "You should know, Eliza Jane, that if you *do* stir up too much trouble, the good sheriff has authorized me—as his deputy, of course—to spank you in lieu of shooting you."

He walked away, leaving her stuttering and brimming with righteous indignation. *Spank* her?

Eliza Jane stomped her foot, so mad she wanted to spit. And as she walked quickly back to the hotel, she fanned her hot face, telling herself it was anger alone that had her so flustered.

If Will Martinson ever *dared* try to bend her over his knee, she'd find herself a good sharp knife, and he could learn how it felt to be a woman.

Four days later...

Oh, the *hell* with spanking. If ever a woman deserved to be shot, it was Eliza Jane Carter.

Will pointed at her, sitting there on the red velvet cushion, thinking she ought to be damn glad it was his finger and not his pistol. "You! Get yourself out of here and leave these whores alone or I will throw you over my shoulder and carry you out."

She had the gall to smile at him—that smile that made his teeth clench in frustration and his balls ache with their own brand of frustration. "Why, Doctor Martinson, I do believe you asked me to initiate a conversation with one of these ladies."

"I asked you to *discreetly* talk to Sadie about getting out of whoring. I did not ask you to talk them *all* out of whoring! Do you know how temperamental cowboys get when every one of them is riding all day with a cockstand he can't shake? Adam had to shoot *two* men just last night."

Eliza Jane cocked an eyebrow at him. *Hellfire*, she had pretty eyes. "I regret the need to be indelicate, but there are ways a man can find his own sexual release, *Doctor*. Neither I nor these women are responsible for their behavior."

"We're knittin' woolens to sell to the cowboys," Fiona chirped. She was young and none too book smart, but she'd established herself as a favorite among the cowboys...and other men in town. Will was especially fond of how flexible she was. "And iffen our cowboys don't want 'em, Miss Carter's gonna ship 'em north to sell."

Will yanked his hat off and ran his hand through his hair in exasperation. "The cowboys don't pay you to knit, they pay you to fuck."

Eliza Jane leapt to her feet, unmindful of the ball of yarn that fell and rolled away. "Doctor Martinson, I will not have you use such language in the presence of these ladies."

"They ain't ladies," he shouted. "They're whores."

"William James Martinson, you get in here right now!" The woman's voice came from a back bedroom, and Will groaned.

Then he pointed his finger at Eliza Jane again. "Now look what you've done. I told you what would happen, woman. When I'm done here I'm going to bend you over my knee, throw up your skirts, and spank you until your ass is as red as a cherry."

"I charge a dollar extra for that," Fiona told Eliza Jane as Will walked like a condemned man down the gaudily decorated hallway.

Miss Adele reigned in all her glory from her bed. She'd been ordered there by Will on account of her health, but she didn't see any reason to let herself go.

Over the top of the red satin sheet, a panel of black lace and ribbons barely constrained the finest, largest breasts a man had ever seen. Her lip rouge accented a pucker made for pleasing a man, and her waves of auburn hair were swept up to accent her graceful neck. She was slowly dying, and yet she remained the strongest, most desirable women he'd ever met.

"Good afternoon, Miss Adele. How you feeling today?"

"Are you insulting my chickens?"

Will managed to kill the smile that threatened to get him in a whole lot more trouble. She wasn't amused, and therefore he wouldn't be either. "I apologize, but they're *knitting*. That infernal woman is going to be the ruin of you, and I won't let that happen."

She tried to laugh, but didn't have the air for it. She coughed instead, waving him away when he bent to listen to her chest. He felt the knot of a whole lot of emotions in his gut as he sat on the edge of the bed.

He loved this whorehouse madam like he'd loved no other woman but his own mother. Seeing her like this damn near killed him, and he'd be goddamned if that crazy man-hater was going to add to her anxiety. He'd save Adam the bullet and shoot her himself before he let Miss Adele come to any harm.

"William, I got more money stashed away than half the big ranch outfits in Texas. I can survive my chickens taking a little vacation. Sometimes they're like children, you see. They've got their mind set on something and it's easier to let them have their head and get it out of their blood than to try to persuade them otherwise."

"She's got no right interfering in your business."

"William, darlin', who do you think paid for those knitting supplies?"

Damnation, but women never made a lick of sense. "Why would you go and do a damn fool thing like that?"

Miss Adele reached over and squeezed his hand. "Because maybe one of those sweet chickens will find a better way and fly the Coop."

"What if they all fly away and leave you alone?"

"They won't. But even if they did, I'd be all right. Now...don't you go losing your temper with Eliza Jane. She's just trying to do right by those girls."

Will slapped his hat against his leg, aggravated all over again just by the mention of her. "You tell me what the hell's gonna happen to the women whose hopes she's raised up when she gets on that stagecoach and never looks back?"

"Eliza Jane promised them she'd be here at least another week, and I believe her to be a woman of her word."

And goddamn if he didn't have a totally mixed reaction to *that* bit of news.

It was best for everybody if Eliza Jane Carter got on that stage the second it rolled into Gardiner. The townsfolk didn't need stirring up. Adam didn't need another target. Miss Adele, no matter how she claimed otherwise, didn't need a women's libber in her business. And Eliza Jane was hell on his own sanity.

On the other hand, he'd had a strong hankering of late to stroke his way down through those hard, prickly layers of hers and find the soft, passionate woman he suspected she was. It was a damn fool notion, but one that had cost him a few hours of sleep nonetheless.

"Go," Miss Adele said, nudging him with her knee. "Go give her the stern talking to you're composing in that head of yours. Just don't let that sheriff shoot her and everything will come out the way it should be in the end."

He bent to kiss her cheek, then pressed his own to hers for a moment. It was his sneaky way of checking her temperature, and it didn't fool her for a minute.

"Go," she ordered, this time slapping him on the ass. "And be nice to my chickens or you'll be one gelded rooster, you hear?"

Will made his way back to the front parlor in time to see Fiona hold up a misshapen, hole-riddled bit of knitting that could have been a sock, a mitten or a saddle for all he could tell.

"This is hard," she whined. "I make more money by just spreading my legs and lettin' the cowboys bounce up and down a few times."

Eliza Jane had taken up her own knitting again, resolutely clacking the needles together, but Will could see the high color in her cheeks. "Yes, Fiona," she said, "but this way you can hold up your head while you're spending your money."

Fiona snorted. "Gardiner ain't like those hoity-toity places back East. I don't reckon I'm too welcome at services on Sunday, but Mr. Dunbarton over at the Mercantile treats me real nice and likes my money just fine. He even gives me a discount on account of my letting him tickle my feet."

Gasps of outrage filled the room. "You get a discount? I let that bastard spend himself all over my prettiest slippers and I had to pay full price for that lace I just bought!"

Once they got going, Miss Adele's chickens could cluck at each other for damn near forever, so Will stepped forward and cleared his throat. "Eliza Jane, I want you in my office in one hour."

She smiled ever so sweetly at him. "I do appreciate the offer, but I'm afraid I must decline. I have a previous engagement."

"One hour," Will warned through gritted teeth. "And if I have to come and get you, there'll be a show the likes of which this town has never seen. Hell, they'll probably even write songs about the day the women's libber got herself spanked right in front of God and Gardiner, Texas."

Chapter Three

Will was mildly surprised to hear the door to his office swing open at the designated time. Truth be told, he was a mite relieved, as well. He'd had some serious doubts as to whether the woman would show up.

Threatening to spank a woman in the middle of the street and actually doing it were two different things altogether. That was the sort of thing that would seriously rile up the good Christian women in town. And he'd rather be set upon by a passel of Adele's clucking chickens than by the ladies of the Gardiner Bible Brigade.

Eliza Jane paused in the doorway, the blazing sun behind her, and Will set his newspaper down across his lap. She sure was a fine-looking woman. It really was too bad about her disposition.

She walked into his office with her chin hiked up. "Doctor Martinson, this is my traveling companion, Edgar Whittemore."

That's when Will noticed the man who'd come in behind her. Once the man closed the door, he stepped out from behind Eliza Jane and Will fought hard not to smile. He hoped Edgar Whittemore wasn't her idea of protection.

The man was built like a barrel softened by wood rot, and he'd already had to push his spectacles back up onto his nose. His brown hair had been spit-combed flat to his head, and he gave the overall impression of being a man who'd left his balls back in his mama's apron pocket.

"Pleased to make your acquaintance," Will said, but he neither rose from his seat nor offered his hand, just in case Edgar's palms were as sweaty as his nose.

"I wish I could say the same, Doctor," the man replied, but the whiny pitch made him sound like a petulant child, so Will wasn't too concerned about the words coming out of his mouth. "Your behavior toward Mrs. Carter has been nothing short of abominable, sir."

"Well, now, that's a mighty big word, Edgar. Good thing I got me one of those paper certificates from Harvard Medical School."

That got their attention. Edgar's glasses almost fell off his nose, while Eliza Jane's eyes narrowed thoughtfully.

"Be that as it may," Edgar squeaked, "this treatment of Mrs. Carter simply cannot be tolerated any longer. Threats of physical violence against her person on the part of both the town's law enforcement and its doctor are simply untoward."

Will folded his newspaper, then leaned forward to prop his elbows on his desk. "Well, heaven forbid we should be untoward. Maybe you should write yourself a letter to the governor, Edgar."

The traveling companion's Adam's apple bobbed. As displays of temper went, it wasn't all that impressive. "Doctor Martinson, perhaps we should—"

"Perhaps you should tell me why a woman who's spent four full days telling the women of this town to speak up to their men is standing there silent while you lecture me on my abominable behavior?"

She wasn't remaining silent by choice, Will figured. Everything about her body language and the expression she was trying like hell to mask let him know Eliza Jane wanted to shove Edgar's head down into his neck until he was just a pair of spectacles perched on two shoulders. He knew the feeling.

"Due to the aforementioned threats of violence," Edgar said, "I felt a man to man discussion was called for—an issue of Mrs. Carter's safety, you understand."

Will tried to stare him down, but the man's gaze was as squirrelly as a preacher in a whorehouse. Finally, he just looked down at the man's city boots. "Rattlesnake!"

Edgar let loose with an unholy, high-pitched squeal that like to wake the dead, then he spun on his heel. After shoving Eliza Jane to one side, causing her to trip over Will's exam stool and go skirt up on the floor, he ripped open the door and fled the office.

Much to Will's dismay, Eliza Jane quickly set her skirts to rights. Without waiting for him to offer assistance, she climbed to her feet and righted the stool.

"That was plain mean," she told him, but he could see a smile dancing around the corners of her mouth.

"Fine choice of a man to see to your physical safety, darlin'."

She took a seat on the wooden bench he kept for waiting patients. "He works for the man who administers my mother's estate, the money from which enables me to travel and further the cause of women's independence."

"So he tugs the purse strings and you have to dance. There's a mighty helping of irony in that."

"I'm so pleased it amuses you."

"Well, you ain't exactly gone out of your way to endear yourself to the citizens of this town," Will explained. "Before you talk about being mean, you should take a good, hard look in the mirror."

"I am *not* mean."

He leaned forward across the desk. "You talked Miss Adele's whores into going on strike, then convinced more than half the women in this town to stop seeing to their men's needs. From a male point of view, that's not just mean. That's downright cruel."

And she knew it, too. He could see by the gleam in her pretty blue eyes that she knew the fastest way to bring a domesticated man to his knees was to cut him off from good food and his warm, willing woman.

The pounding of running feet approaching on the plank sidewalk caught his attention. Whoever it was was moving too quickly to be Edgar Whittemore coming back for the charge he'd abandoned.

Johnny Barnes ran through the open door, his face red and his chest heaving, carrying his baby wrapped in a blanket.

"Doc! Jesus, you gotta help me, Doc!"

Will moved around the desk and took Johnny Junior before his father could drop him on the floor. "What happened?"

"His britches..." Relieved of his burden, Johnny paused to bend at the waist and take a few deep breaths. "I was trying to change his britches, and what's in there...it can't be right, Doc. He must be sick or something."

Will laid the nine-month old on the exam table and peeled back the blanket. Then he gagged as an aroma like a three-day-dead skunk filled his office. He, a Harvard educated doctor and a veteran of the Union's hospital tents, swiped at the tears blurring his vision and gagged again.

"Good lord, Johnny, he ain't sick. He's ripe is what he is."

"Are you trying to tell me that's normal?"

"It started out as normal, but this ain't like cheese or wine that gets better with age. Did Melinda take sick to bed?"

He worked efficiently as he spoke, cleaning the baby and rediapering him from his own stock. The office was going to be a while airing out before he could close his door, though.

"She ain't in bed," Johnny answered. "That crazy woman done moved in to the hotel until I show her some appreciation. If that ain't the most damn fool notion."

Will turned and pinned Eliza Jane with a look that would have made a woman with a weaker constitution squirm. This one only glared right back at him.

"It's all that damn women's libber's fault," Johnny continued, still oblivious to her presence. "Save us all a whole lick of trouble if Sheriff Caldwell would just shoot her and be done with it."

"He'd like to," Eliza Jane said, and Johnny damn near jumped out of his skin. "But murder's not a good choice for an officer of the law."

"You!" Johnny bellowed, and Johnny Junior, being startled out of the euphoria of having clean britches, started to fuss. "This is all your fault."

Will picked up the baby and leaned against the wall to watch the show. "Eliza Jane Carter, this here's Johnny Barnes from down to the livery stable. Johnny, meet the damn women's libber."

She stood and Will got the impression she was accustomed to using her height to intimidate men. She had a good five inches or so on Johnny. "Your lack of appreciation for your wife is hardly my fault, Mr. Barnes."

"If you hadn't come here, Melinda would be home right now taking care of Johnny Junior."

"And you. Taking care of you."

"Well, yeah, I reckon." Johnny looked downright confused. "She takes care of me, too."

"And do you ever bring her flowers? Have you ever thanked her for the meals she cooks or for having a clean shirt to wear?"

He frowned and scratched his head. "When's the last time she thanked me for sweating my balls off—excuse my language, ma'am—every day at the livery to feed her and this young'un and keep a roof over their heads?"

"She thanks you hundreds of times a day, in all the little things she does for you," Eliza Jane argued, and Will just shook his head. "Cooking, cleaning, mending, raising your son and seeing to your needs."

Johnny's face turned as red as Miss Adele's satin sheets. "It ain't right for you to be talkin' about a man's needs, Miss Carter. That ain't right at all. My mama's got a word for women like you."

"Whoa!" Will stepped between them, holding the baby out to his father. "Now, Johnny, there's no call to bring your mama into this situation."

Lucy Barnes was the righteousness-spewing, book-thumping, self-proclaimed leader of the Gardiner Bible Brigade, and Will wanted no truck with her. She was one *hell* of a scary woman.

"We were doin' just fine, Doc. Melinda and I had a nice life together before *she* came to town. Now my wife's living in the hotel and Junior here misses his mama something fierce."

"Your wife wouldn't have moved out if she was happy," Eliza Jane argued, and Will winced.

"You watch yourself, lady," Johnny said. "Or somebody just might save Sheriff Caldwell the cost of a bullet."

He left, the baby cheerfully waving bye-bye over his shoulder. Will decided to go on back to his desk and sit down before he throttled Eliza Jane in his own office.

"Close the door," he told her, despite the lingering odor.

She looked for a second like she wanted to force a *please* out of him, but she closed the door and took a seat on the bench again.

"These people aren't chess pieces that you can move around for your amusement," he told her. "You're playing with people's *lives*."

"I assure you, Doctor Martinson, that I am neither playing nor amused."

"Now there's no call to get all prissy with me. We're just having a conversation."

Eliza Jane folded her hands in her lap. "It seems our conversations consist of you telling me what to do and expecting me to do it. I'm sure you're aware of my feeling regarding women blindly obeying men."

He was definitely aware that he found it sexy, the way she pursed her lips when she was trying to be prim and proper. "Maybe it would help some if you think of me as the deputy sheriff and yourself as the town troublemaker."

"I'm not surprised you find a woman with a mind of her own troublesome, Deputy."

Will wasn't of a mind to talk circles with this woman for the rest of the day. "What happened to *Mister* Carter?"

Eliza Jane sucked in a surprised breath and Will was pleased he'd thrown her off her guard. And while he had to admit to a certain amount of personal curiosity, that wasn't why he'd asked.

"I don't believe my marriage is any of your concern," she replied stiffly.

"Right now you're stirring up trouble in my town, so everything about you is my business. Unless you'd rather I fetch Sheriff Caldwell."

She gave him a hateful look, twisting her fingers together in her lap. "My husband divorced me because I couldn't bear him a child. He cast me aside as though I'm worthless because I'm barren."

Will's professional interest was stampeded over by the personal when he saw how the anger he heard in her voice couldn't keep the pain from her eyes. "He was a jackass."

He saw the sheen of tears, surprised because she didn't seem the weepy kind.

"My father supported his decision."

"If that's the case, he's a jackass, too," Will replied. "And the problem might have been with your husband, darlin'. Being a doctor, I know these things."

"His new wife bore him two children in three years, and she was expecting again when I left Philadelphia."

"He's still a jackass for not seeing there's so much more to you than a barren womb. He was a fool not to see that."

She was looking everywhere but at his face. "If we're finished discussing the humiliating, intimate details of my life, I'd like to leave now."

Will had thought he'd like Eliza Jane more if she was less prickly, but he didn't like seeing her like this any better. "What I was trying to get at is maybe you're not spreading any message but your own personal bitterness."

Outrage flamed on her cheeks and Will had to bite back a smile. It seemed he liked her more when she was fired up, after all.

"How *dare* you?" She rose to her feet, using her height again, and he didn't bother telling her it had no effect on him. He just folded his arms across his chest and looked up at her.

"Hit a sore spot, did I, darlin'? I can't help thinking if your husband hadn't divorced you, you wouldn't be traveling around preaching the evils of men."

"I don't preach the evils of men. I preach the strength of women." Eliza Jane leaned over his desk, placing her palms on the wood. The position put him close to eye level with her breasts, but Will tried to pay attention. "And perhaps it was being thrown away like a broken toy that opened my eyes to the fact that a woman has no standing but what the man in her life—father or husband—chooses to allow her."

She sucked in a breath after that tirade and Will's gaze was drawn back to her breasts. Did the woman even know what she was doing to him?

"The way women are regarded in this country is wrong," she said, really on a roll. "And if the men in this town are threatened by a woman speaking her mind, then they're in the wrong, too."

"I agree," Will said.

She'd been working up a full head of steam, but his words derailed her. "And...you do?"

"Yes, I do." He felt a pang of regret when she stood up straight again, removing her breasts from his close proximity.

"But not everybody in Gardiner does. Plus there are a lot of women who are impressed by what you're saying but don't have the education or experience, and they can be mighty clumsy in trying to practice what it is you're preaching."

"But if it changes their—"

"Johnny and Melinda Barnes did have a good life going, Eliza Jane. They were a happy, loving couple, been sweethearts since they were walking barefoot and hand-in-hand to the schoolhouse. And that baby was a joyous occasion, let me tell you.

"And I'm willing to wager the only reason Melinda up and left her two Johnnys is your words getting all mixed up in her head, making her think she's supposed to be holding out for more. And there ain't no more she needs than a husband who loves her, a healthy baby and their little home she's got done up real nice."

He had to give her credit for giving his words due consideration before she spoke again. "I'll talk to Melinda Barnes privately. If my words have misguided her, as you believe, I'll help her sort things out and get her home to her family."

"Thank you, darlin'." He grinned at her just because he liked the way it flustered her. "And if you could try not to cause any more discontent before the stage comes, I'd be mighty grateful."

He didn't like to think about her leaving so soon. It was a foolish notion, but he really wanted to get to know her better.

And just not getting to know what was under her clothes, either, although he wouldn't mind that.

Will considered himself a smart man, and he knew Gardiner wouldn't hold a woman like Eliza Jane for long. But it wouldn't break his heart any if the stage was late, sensible or not.

"I don't deliberately set out to cause discontent." Her highly attractive mouth curved into a small smile. "It just sort of...happens. I have that effect on people, I guess."

That wasn't the effect she had on *him*, at all, but he reckoned she didn't want to hear about the baser biological urges of a man right then.

"Just try to lie low until the stage comes, darlin'. If you lie low, things will quiet down."

಑೮ನಿೲಅ

It was standing room only in the front parlor of the Gardiner Hotel the following evening, but it was deathly silent when Eliza Jane finished speaking.

She wasn't surprised. Very few women were accustomed to hearing their monthly cycles spoken about at all, never mind with such frankness. A handful of women had even fled the room at different points. But if even one woman managed to give her body a few months' rest between pregnancies, it was worth the scandalized, stunned silence of her audience.

Dan O'Brien—who as it turned out was not only the desk clerk, but the proprietor of the establishment—had tried to protest having a lecture in his front parlor, but Eliza Jane had simply informed him of the evening's topic and he'd fled for parts unknown.

"Any questions?" she asked, and she was surprised when a young woman shyly raised her hand. It was the pregnant woman she'd seen when she first arrived in town, the one who had an infant and toddler already.

"But, Miss Carter, Genesis 3:16 tells us 'in sorrow thou shalt bring forth children, and thy desire shall be to thy husband, and he shall rule over thee', and Ephesians 5:22 says 'Wives, submit yourselves unto your own husbands, as unto the Lord.'"

This was always the trickiest part of her lectures. If she tried to refute the word of God she'd lose them, and every word she'd said would be ignored. If she totally ceded to the scripture, her lecture would be dismissed as impossible to apply to their own lives.

"That's why you need to talk to your husbands," Eliza Jane answered, causing a lot of fidgeting in the room. "I know it's awkward, but your health is important. Tell *them* what I've told you about the toll repeated pregnancies takes on a woman's body. And if that doesn't work, remind them that if they wear out your bodies, they get to raise the children you've already had all by themselves."

Scattered laughter broke some of the tension and the women got bolder about asking questions. She spent another half-hour answering them.

As she spoke, her awareness of a certain woman in the crowd grew. It was hard to tell her age, worn and beat by the sun as she was, but Eliza Jane guessed she was in her late forties. And she was scared.

The woman's eyes as she watched the lecture were incredibly sad, but her body language hinted to Eliza Jane that the very last thing that woman wanted was to be caught there.

She'd seen it before, and it both enraged her and broke her heart knowing this woman probably lived in fear of the very man who had vowed to love and protect her until death they did part.

Eliza Jane decided she'd seek the woman out before leaving town. It shouldn't be too hard to find out who she was, even without asking Will or the sheriff—in her past experience, involving the law in domestic matters such as this was disastrous. She'd talk to the woman herself.

Halfway through a discussion on a method of stopping pregnancy an older woman had learned from her grandfather's slave mistress, the front door of the hotel opened with a bang and Sheriff Caldwell strode into the room.

"I've got a crowd of menfolk getting drunker and madder by the second and children who need minding. It's time for you ladies to go on home now."

"Sheriff Caldwell," Eliza Jane said in a voice loud enough to still the women who'd already begun to gather their things. "We have a right to assemble here."

He turned his cold, dark gaze on her. "You've caused enough trouble for tonight."

"I am *not* causing trouble. I am conducting a meeting, which is well within my rights."

The sheriff stalked across the room, advancing on her like a black panther moving in for the kill. When he drew his pistol, every woman in the room—including Eliza Jane—gasped.

She'd suffered a great many indignities in her work, but she'd never had an officer of the law pull a gun on her. Eliza Jane straightened her shoulders and lifted her chin to show she wouldn't be intimidated so easily. It was time to practice what she preached.

"Sheriff, I don't—"

"You are disturbing the peace in my town, lady," he interrupted. "And many a people—well, the ones who ain't dead, anyway—will tell you I don't take kindly to having my peace disturbed."

There was now a hurried, but nearly silent, exodus of women out the front door, which made Eliza Jane want to stomp her foot in vexation. How could the men of Gardiner be expected to treat their women with any sort of decency when their own sheriff was a violent, pigheaded boor?

Suddenly a ripple of excitement ran through the line of women. "Lucy Barnes is coming!"

Sheriff Caldwell turned as pale as flour and shoved his gun back into its holster. "Oh shit—excuse the language, ladies."

He made a break for the kitchen—and the hotel's back door, presumably—but he stumbled over a dainty parlor chair and crashed to the floor in a tangle of splintered wood and some curses Eliza Jane had never even heard before. The man actually scrambled a few feet on his hands and feet before managing to get up and run. A few seconds later, the screen door of the kitchen closed with a bang.

Well, wasn't *that* interesting? Clearly this Lucy Barnes— who she'd heard described as the moral compass of the town— was somebody she needed to make an ally of.

A Bible-bearing woman with a face as red as apples and a body built like the tree they'd fallen from stepped through the front door. She pointed a trembling finger at Eliza Jane and screamed at the top of her considerable lungs, "*Jezebel!*"

Unlike the sheriff, Eliza Jane didn't trip over a single chair on her way out the back door.

Chapter Four

"*This* is your idea of lying low? You can't hide in my office forever, Eliza Jane," Will pointed out when he was through laughing so hard his stomach hurt.

"She called me Jezebel," Eliza Jane protested. She did look a little shaken, but Lucy was known to have that effect on people.

"Sweetheart, I've only known you a week and I can safely hazard a guess that's not the worst thing you've ever been called."

She crossed her arms, emphasizing those beautiful breasts he'd spent way too much time thinking about of late. "Admittedly, that's true, but I thought she would be an ally of sorts when I saw the effect her name had on Sheriff Caldwell."

"Lucy Barnes *is* about the only person I've ever met who scares Adam."

"I'm sure she, being a Christian woman, disapproves of his shooting people—and brandishing his weapon in a gathering of women."

"Oh, it ain't the shooting people that bothers her. She's got her mind set on him marrying her daughter."

48

Will relished the rare moments he managed to render her speechless. She was twice as pretty when she was quiet.

Unfortunately those moments never lasted long. "You can't be serious. Can you even imagine what a child of that man and that woman's daughter would be like? It's little wonder he's scared."

That *was* a little frightening, come to think of it. "I don't think he's gotten as far as pondering offspring. He gets about as far as having Lucy Barnes as a mother-in-law and heads for the bottom of a bottle."

"Why would she want the sheriff for her daughter instead of you?"

Well, if that didn't just make a man feel warm inside—*real* warm. "So you'd rather marry me than Adam, would you?"

Her eyes got big and her cheeks rosy. "I would rather not marry either of you, under any circumstances. I simply meant that your prospects as a doctor seem more attractive to the mother of a marriageable girl than those of a crazy sheriff."

"She doesn't think I'm good enough for her daughter, on account of how much time I spend at the Chicken Coop."

"Why wouldn't she feel the same way about Sheriff Caldwell?"

"Oh, Adam won't step foot in the Coop. Won't have anything to do with whores in general. We figure *that*, along with his not having a wife, is why he's so quick on the trigger when it comes to shooting people."

"Oh, I just assumed..." Her words trailed off and she narrowed her eyes at him. "Just how much time *do* you spend at the Chicken Coop?"

"Enough to learn a whole lot about women they don't teach at Harvard."

She wanted to be scandalized, but he could see by her expression she was more intrigued than anything. Outrage may have explained some of the color in her cheeks, but not her quickened breath or the little flick of her tongue over her bottom lip.

There was no point in trying to deny to himself he'd developed a powerful hunger for this woman, but he wasn't sure just how liberated she was about these things. If he kissed her right here and now, would she return the favor, or slap his face?

When footsteps stopped outside his door, Will cursed while Eliza Jane yelped and ducked behind his examination curtain. He yanked it closed just as the office door opened.

"That surely is a nasty rash you've got there," he called back over his shoulder, just to make it look good, of course.

Hellfire and damnation personified stepped into his office and Will smiled. "Good evening, Mrs. Barnes."

"Did that brazen hussy come here?"

"Considering how few women in this town—or any other place, for that matter—have achieved your level of moral fortitude, I'm afraid I'll have to ask you to be more specific."

She narrowed her eyes and shook the good Book at him. "Don't you sass me, boy. I know you've been keeping time with Eliza Jane Carter."

Oh boy, things were getting interesting. But if the pain-in-the-ass woman behind the curtain didn't know enough to keep her mouth shut, they'd get downright ugly. Mrs. Barnes wasn't a person who stood for having her feathers ruffled "The sheriff asked me to keep an eye on her while she's in town—make sure she doesn't cause too much trouble."

"That better be all there is to it, or I'll make sure the only doctoring you get to do is turning breeched calves."

Will stuck his thumbs in his pockets and rocked back on his heels. "Yes, ma'am. And speaking of the sheriff, has Beth Ann found herself a husband yet?"

He half-expected lightning bolts to shoot from her eyes and sear him on the spot. "Don't you worry none about my Beth Ann. Once Sheriff Caldwell tastes my girl's apple pie, he won't settle for anybody else."

Knowing Lucy Barnes, she'd probably hexed the apples somehow. He'd have to warn Adam against eating any wayward pies.

"If I see Mrs. Carter, I'll be sure to let her know you're looking for her and that she should stop by your home for some of that delicious lemonade of yours."

Since the Barnes family could afford good, white sugar—and she wanted everybody to know it—Lucy made lemonade so sweet it made a man's teeth ache. Adam had been forced to drink gallons of it before he started getting more adept at avoiding her.

"That woman's not welcome under my roof," she hissed. "You just tell her I'm keeping my eye on her. On *both* of you."

She left in a cloud of righteousness that made Will want to choke. Someday soon that woman needed to be put in her place.

"Is she gone?" Eliza Jane whispered urgently.

He slipped behind the curtain, then shook his head at her worried expression. "How is it that you can stick that pretty little nose up at an armed man, but that one woman has you shaking in your shoes?"

"That one woman even scares the armed man in question, so don't you dare laugh at me."

"You sure do have a knack for getting people all riled up."

"Some people need to be."

"You get *me* all riled up," he said, letting the heat he felt inside seep into his voice. It was a dangerous ember he was poking at, but he suspected if he could fan that smoldering spark of hers into a flame, she'd burn with a passion that would leave them both scorched and breathless.

And she hadn't missed his meaning, judging by the way she was chewing at her bottom lip. "I'm sure any one of Miss Adele's chickens would be happy to smooth your feathers."

She missed derisive by a mile, Will thought. She sounded more like a jealous lover. He moved closer to her, just short of crowding her. "I haven't visited the Coop in that capacity since you came to town, darlin'. The chickens can't scratch the itch I got."

Her blue eyes got so big he thought he'd drown in them, but she didn't say a word.

"What about you, Eliza Jane? You got an itch you need scratched?"

He watched her throat work as she swallowed, then shook her head too quickly. "I guess that particular itch just faded right away since scratching it wasn't worth the bother."

"Oh, darlin'. If that's really the case, your husband wasn't doing it right."

Her cheeks flushed, and in the dim light of the lamp, her eyes glittered. "It's rather a simple procedure, *Doctor*, so I doubt he was performing it incorrectly.

He grinned and stepped even closer to her, definitely in crowding territory now. "If you can use words like procedure and performing, he for damn sure wasn't doing it correctly."

Will knew his way around a woman well enough to know this one was affected by him in a very good way. And he'd bet if he pressed his lips to that sweet spot on her neck, he'd feel her pulse fluttering like a hummingbird's.

He cupped the side of her face with one palm. Her eyelids slid closed and she sighed, turning her face into his hand. "Did you do that when he touched you?"

She shook her head slightly, barely moving. With his other hand, he took hold of her clenched fist. As her hand relaxed, he threaded his fingers through hers and raised it so he could kiss each knuckle. Eliza Jane's entire body shuddered, and the heated blush of her face crept downward, disappearing into the stiff collar of her blouse.

That collar wasn't the only thing stiff. When she sucked her bottom lip in and started worrying at it with her teeth, Will almost groaned out loud. And shifting his feet around didn't do a damn thing to ease the almost painful pressure below his belt.

"Making love ain't about performing a procedure, darlin'. It's about pleasure."

Her sweet bottom lip slid free of her teeth and Will moved in, pressing his mouth to hers before they could capture it again. Her lips were soft and willing under his, and he deepened the kiss. She gasped when his tongue brushed over hers, and this time Will *did* groan.

He left her mouth, blazing a trail of kisses to her jaw, and he spoke against her skin. "And when your woman has her legs wrapped around your waist and her hips lifted off the bed...when she's got one hand raking the skin off your back..."

She whimpered, and Will tipped her chin back to expose her throat. He licked a trail of moisture down to the collar of her blouse and then blew gently on her overheated flesh. "...and the other hand is holding a pillow to her mouth so her screaming doesn't wake the whole damn town and she can't even talk because it's all she can do to breathe..."

He nipped at her jaw and her whole body jumped. "Then, darlin'...*then* you know you're doing it right."

She was panting now, and Will brought his lips to her ear, inhaling the sweet scent of her hair. "Have you ever felt like that, Eliza Jane?"

"No," she said, and her voice was small and breathless.

Will lifted his head and saw the hunger in her eyes. "I want to make you feel it. I want to see the woman behind the starch and all those buttons."

He ran his hands over her hips and pulled her close, nestling the proof of just how badly he wanted her against the juncture of her thighs. And when Eliza Jane lifted one knee, running the inside of her thigh up the outside of his, he damn near came undone.

"I want to strip you naked, sweetheart." He wrapped his hand around the back of her neck and hauled her into another kiss—this one not as sweet and gentle. She hooked her leg around the back of his knee, arching her hips against his.

"I want to touch every part of you," he told her, inching his mouth down toward that top button again. "I want to kiss every part of you. I want to *taste* you."

"Yes," she breathed, and Will felt like his whole body had just been set on fire.

He ran his fingers up over her ribs, finally cupping the weight of her breasts in his hands. It was time for the clothes to go. "I'm going to—"

"Doc!"

Eliza Jane jerked like she'd been stuck with a fork, and a mouthful of curses rattled around in Will's brain. "*What?*"

"Davey got himself kicked by that ornery mule of his," the intruder called through the curtain.

"Can't it wait?" Will asked for the first time in all his years in Gardiner. Eliza Jane was untangling herself from him and he didn't want to let her go.

"You'd best come now. His balls are swelling up as big as a bull's!"

Will cared a lot more about his own balls right then, but Eliza Jane was already smoothing her hair and the moment had passed on.

"You know, darlin'," he whispered, "if that itch gets bad enough, you might wanna see a doctor about getting it scratched."

Then he snuck through the curtain and walked—very stiffly—over to his medical bag.

ഓഇഐ

Edgar Whittemore was lying in wait for Eliza Jane in the lobby of the hotel. As her body was still reliving the glorious feeling of Will Martinson's hands and her mind was trying to focus on the stage's arrival in three days, she nearly walked right into him.

She considered walking right past him. She didn't want to talk to him right now. She wanted to be alone so she could think about the doctor. But she knew from experience he wouldn't stop pestering her until she'd addressed his concerns.

"Hello, Edgar."

"How do you expect me to fulfill my duties as your chaperone if you continually sneak out of the hotel without informing me of your agenda?" he demanded in a voice that grated across her nerves like a wide-toothed comb across a violin's strings.

"I didn't sneak. I walked down the stairs, through the lobby and out the front door. If you spent more time paying attention and less time checking your clothes for scorpions, you'd have seen me."

"I have asked you before not to schedule a lecture without my knowledge."

"And I have told you before your presence drives women away." While she was referring to her lectures, of course, she also wasn't surprised he'd never had a wife.

"Mrs. Carter!" Dan, the hotel clerk, stepped up to her without looking her in the eye. He was, no doubt, afraid she might have the indecency to mention the female cycle in his establishment again. "I got a telegram for you."

She took the slip of paper and thanked him. Edgar cleared his throat, reminding her in his less-than-subtle, phlegmy manner they were in the middle of a conversation he probably considered important. But she rarely received telegrams, and never one bearing good news.

Good for nothing husband gambled away all my money. Stop. Then he gambled away all yours. Stop. Got himself killed. Stop. Good luck. Stop. B. Millar.

Decorum be damned. She collapsed onto one of the parlor chairs and put her head down between her knees, sucking in deep breaths that still weren't deep enough. The slip of paper slid from her fingers, and she didn't bother protesting when Edgar picked it up. A moment later he sank down onto a chair next to her and she had no idea which of them was making the distressed whimpering sounds.

"Mrs. Carter, are you okay?" Dan was saying. So it was her, then. "Do you need the Doc?"

She shook her head frantically. Good Lord, the last person she needed right now was Will Martinson.

All of her money was gone—money left to her by her mother, who had inherited it from *her* mother. All gone. In trying to protect the money from the men in Eliza Jane's life, her mother had entrusted it to a man with a gambling problem.

Rage sizzled through her. If she had been allowed control of her own inheritance, this wouldn't have happened. She was considered too delicate, too weak-minded to tend to her own finances? At least she didn't squander away somebody else's money.

A hand patted her back and Eliza Jane lifted her head to find Edgar trying in his awkward way to console her. She sighed. While he was a most vexing travel companion, they had been together for several years. And his situation was now as desperate as hers.

"What are we going to do?" she whispered.

He took a deep breath and pushed his glasses back up onto the bridge of his nose. "We'll simply use our remaining funds to travel back to Philadelphia. Once there, maybe we can discover the details of this unfortunate incident and perhaps find some legal recourse."

Eliza Jane nodded, her mind latching onto the plan. "Yes. There must be some recourse. There are laws governing these sorts of affairs."

Of course, the person who'd broken the laws was dead, and his estate apparently decimated alongside her own, but it was a goal to work toward.

"Here's what we're going to do," Edgar said in a strangely calm and decisive voice. "We're going to retire for the evening. After a good night's sleep, we'll meet at the restaurant for breakfast at eight and talk more about what we should do, such as sending letters on ahead to help expedite the process."

Eliza Jane nodded and rose to her feet, feeling only a little shaky in the knees. "Yes, let's do that."

They parted ways, and though Eliza Jane tried to follow his advice, sleep remained elusive until the wee hours. Every time she willfully tried not to think about her new state of poverty, she ended up remembering the feel of Will's mouth against hers, of his hands against her flesh. Forcibly, she turned her mind away from those images, only to find herself dwelling again on her financial situation.

Edgar's solution—getting on the next stage and returning to Philadelphia—was her only reasonable option. But there was a part of her already regretting not knowing how things would turn out with Sadie's child, or how the chickens would fare when Miss Adele passed on. She wanted to know how Lucy

Barnes was going to get the sheriff to the altar with her daughter. And she wanted to spend more time with Will. As she finally drifted off to sleep, she thought it was a shame she couldn't stay in Gardiner just a little longer.

By eight-fifteen the next morning, she was getting nervous. Edgar was *never* late. By eight-thirty, she was growing frantic, and by a quarter til nine, she was knocking on the door of his room. There was no answer.

After knocking several more times in vain, she went down to the front desk. "Have you seen Mr. Whittemore?"

Dan's Adam's apple bobbed as he swallowed hard. "He checked out, ma'am. Told me he was buying a horse and leaving town."

Dread curdled like day-old sour milk in Eliza Jane's stomach. "He can't just up and leave town. Not without me."

"I'm sure sorry, Mrs. Carter, but he paid for your room here for a month and left you this note."

There was nothing she could do to hide the trembling of her hand from him as she took the note and unfolded it.

As my employer is deceased and no further funds are forthcoming, I consider my employment hereby terminated. I have paid for your lodging through the month. I regret I cannot leave you further monies, but as I am entitled to severance compensation, I have dispersed the remaining funds to myself. Best wishes, E. Whittemore.

Not Edgar, too. This simply couldn't be happening. She was stranded in Gardiner, Texas with not so much as a dollar to her name.

Eliza Jane crumpled the paper in her fist and spun on her heel. She imagined the clunking of her heels as a war drum as she marched toward the sheriff's office, not even registering the people on the street, even the angry men in pink shirts.

Chapter Five

Will finished the piss-poor coffee Adam had offered him and considered getting on with his day. He had a shipment of medications to inventory and letters from an East Coast colleague to answer, and he wasn't going to get it done sitting in the sheriff's office.

"There's something in the air today, Doc," Adam said. "Can't rightly say what, but I've got a bad feeling."

"I'm sure whatever it is, you'll just shoot it." Will hoped like hell whatever it was had nothing to do with Eliza Jane.

"Probably so." Adam stood and adjusted his gun belt. "Let's go get some breakfast. I hate killing people on an empty stomach."

It took Will a few seconds to grab his hat and close the door behind him, and then he almost ran right into Adam. The sheriff had stopped in the middle of the sidewalk and shoved his hat back on his head.

"Is it just me, Doc, or do you see a whole lot of angry men wearing pink shirts?"

Aw, hell. "I see them."

"I really wanted some steak and eggs, too."

"Let's go get some. Ain't no law being broken here. A man's got a right to wear a pink shirt if he's a mind to."

"And half the men in town just happened to get a hankerin' to wear pink on the same day?"

"Maybe they had a sale at the Mercantile."

Adam snorted and fixed his hat. "Or maybe that women's libber of yours is up to no good again."

Will didn't see any point in wasting his breath trying to deny it. This had Eliza Jane's name all over it.

"Oh, hell," Adam muttered, and Will followed his friend's glance to see the woman in question bearing down on them like a runaway freight train. "Let's ignore her and pray she goes away."

Will could have told him it wouldn't work, but he followed him back inside anyway, not bothering to close the door. It wouldn't keep her out. Adam returned to his desk and started reading the paper with a vengeance while Will poured himself another mug of piss-poor coffee and settled in the other chair to wait.

It didn't take long. When Eliza Jane stormed in, her face even more pink than the menfolk's shirts, Adam didn't even glance up. Will would have laughed if she didn't look fit to commit murder at that moment.

"I have somebody I want you to shoot," she told Adam straight out.

That certainly got Will's attention, and the sheriff's, too. "It ain't the doc, is it?"

She looked at Will as though considering. "No."

"Good. I couldn't shoot a friend." He folded the paper and slapped it down on his desk. "If you're having some sort of problem, why don't you just tell him about it? He's a sworn deputy and *he* likes you."

"Because Doctor Martinson is far too civilized for this matter," she said.

Will tried not to be insulted. After all, being called civilized was a compliment as a rule. But the fact she was turning to another man for help set his teeth on edge. And his gun wasn't exactly just for decoration.

"Edgar Whittemore has fled town with all of my money. I want him hunted down and shot like a dog."

Adam took his sweet time considering her words. "I ain't never shot a dog, ma'am. How exactly would that differ from shooting down a man, do you reckon?"

"I don't care *how* you shoot him, as long as it causes him a significant amount of pain."

"Well now," he said so slowly Will wanted to slap him in the back of the head just to make him talk faster, "that's a pretty bloodthirsty way of thinking from a woman who just decked out half the town in pink."

The shirts didn't even come close to the color of Eliza Jane's cheeks, but Will was having a hard time feeling sorry for her. It seemed like every time he and Adam managed to get folks calmed down, she went ahead and got them all riled up again.

"I don't do their laundry," Eliza Jane said.

Will chuckled. "That's one hell of a coincidence, darlin'."

"Sometimes men need to be reminded that the women who make their lives easier can also make it more complicated. I distributed small squares of cloth imbued with red dye. But that's not nearly as urgent a problem as that of Edgar Whittemore."

"The way I see it, that problem's only urgent to you."

"He said your horse was ugly," Eliza Jane said. "I heard him."

Adam raised an eyebrow. "Did he now?"

"He did. Edgar told me your horse was so ugly his own dam probably wouldn't give him milk." And she nodded as she spoke to emphasize the point.

Will tried his damndest not to laugh, but he couldn't hold it back. He knew Eliza Jane had a way of making people listen to her, but this was just downright devious. Unfortunately, he got Adam laughing, too, and that made her so furious she even stomped her foot.

"This is *not* amusing! That man stole from me, and I want you to go and get my money back and then shoot him."

When the men managed to get themselves under control—with help from her downright evil expression—Adam put on his best serious face. "How did Edgar Whittemore come to gain possession of your money?"

"The executor of my mother's estate entrusted it to him in his capacity as my chaperone."

"So he was *supposed* to have your money?"

Eliza Jane took a deep breath. "Yes, but he wasn't *supposed* to run off with it."

"Was he told that specifically?"

When she placed her palms on Adam's desk and leaned forward, Will shook his head. Trying to intimidate the sheriff with her height wouldn't work.

"Sheriff Caldwell," she said in a deceptively quiet voice, "that money is mine. Despite the fact it was administered by two men, those funds belonged solely to me. When Mr. Whittemore severed his employment, he also lost the right to govern my funds."

Will had to admire the short rein she kept on her temper. He also had to admire the way Adam was keeping his gaze anywhere but the breasts Eliza Jane was displaying front and center. Will knew that was no easy feat, and the sheriff was a true friend, for sure.

Of course, thinking about those breasts of hers got Will thinking about the very hot and sweaty dreams he'd been having and wondering if Eliza Jane could afford to leave town now. Maybe she'd have to stick around for a while longer, and wouldn't *that* be both a blessing and a curse?

"Did he leave you anything at all?" Will asked, drawing their attention to him. At least Eliza Jane stood up straight again, removing temptation from Adam's line of sight.

"He had the semblance of decency enough to pay a month in advance for my hotel room. But he absconded with the remaining cash."

"Unfortunately, Mrs. Carter," Adam said, leaning back in his creaky wooden chair, "I ain't sure that's reason enough to shoot a man down like a dog. Or even like a possum, I reckon."

Eliza Jane's fingers curled and Will wondered if she was fixing to try scratching Adam's eyes out. He hoped not.

"You shot a man for calling your horse ugly," she hissed.

"Yes, ma'am, but the facts weren't in question."

"The fact is, your horse is—"

Will leapt to his feet, ready to throw himself in front of the bullet.

"—irrelevant."

Will breathed a sigh of relief and managed to keep himself from strangling her. She shouldn't bait Adam like that.

But she wasn't done yet. "This isn't a matter of equine comeliness. It's a matter of theft."

"I haven't had my breakfast yet," Adam said, and any citizen of Gardiner would have taken that for the warning it was.

"Well, I can't *afford* breakfast, can I?"

Will watched them try to stare each other down, realizing this was the first time he wouldn't put his money on Adam.

All of a sudden, the sheriff grinned. "You have to get a job."

Eliza Jane blinked. "A job?"

"Yes, ma'am. If you ain't got money, that's the best way to get some. You think you're entitled to being treated equal to a man, so now you can work like one. And the men who can give you a job are right outside. Wearing pink shirts, I reckon."

Will would give her one thing—she could cuss like a man when the occasion called for it.

೮೦೮೧೦೪

Eliza Jane tried not to be discouraged as she stepped into the office of the *Gardiner Gazette.* Or more correctly, she tried not to let the discouragement she *did* feel show on her face. The search for employment wasn't going well, and her reputation had proved to precede her.

A young boy setting type looked up her. "Help you?"

"My name is Mrs. Carter. I'd like to speak to the proprietor about any employment opportunities."

The boy's eyes widened. "Jumping Jehosophat! You're that da...you're the women's libber."

She sighed. "I am."

"You want to see who about what?"

"I need a job."

It was at that moment the largest man Eliza Jane had ever seen stepped out of a back room. Big and brawny, with ink-stained fingers like sausages and sporting a mass of unruly black hair on his head and face, he greatly resembled a giant, shaggy grizzly interrupted during his winter nap.

His altogether frightening appearance was in no way mitigated by the very bright and cheery pink shirt he wore.

"Well, well, Mrs. Carter," he said, and she caught a trace of an almost faded accent—English, perhaps. "What an unexpected surprise."

The boy laughed. "If it was expected, it wouldn't be a surprise, would it?"

The man's face reddened to a shade that contrasted horribly with the shirt. "Billy, you go on out back and fix yourself a snack."

Eliza Jane waited until Billy was gone before saying, "I'm sure the surprise isn't entirely welcome, Mr. ..."

"Seymour. Frank Seymour."

He folded his beefy arms across his even beefier chest and waited. Clearly he wasn't inclined to make this visit any easier on her, not that she could blame him.

A shadowy movement behind Mr. Seymour made her suspect Billy was not having the snack he was instructed to eat, but was shamelessly eavesdropping. She had to admit she didn't care for having another witness to her ongoing humiliation, even if he was only half-grown.

Eliza Jane drew a deep breath and straightened her shoulders. "I know you're disinclined to feel kindly toward me just now, Mr. Seymour, but I assure you nothing about my lectures was meant toward you personally."

"Since I'm the one personally wearing pink, I'm *disinclined* to care."

Pride was a difficult lump to swallow but she forced it down. "I'm sorry about the shirts. I really am. But I need a job."

"Even if I had an opening—which I don't—you're the last person I'd offer employment. You wreaked enough havoc before I ever even met you."

That seemed to be the prevailing statement among the male business owners in town. Since only two women owned businesses in Gardiner—Marguerite at over at the restaurant and Miss Adele—her situation seemed hopeless indeed. She wasn't any more suited to cooking and waiting tables than she was to being a prostitute.

"Consider this," she said after a moment. "The faster I earn money, the faster I leave town."

Frank Seymour seemed to consider what she said, but then he shrugged. "As appealing as that sounds, I can barely keep myself in ink as it is. Can't afford any help."

Eliza Jane forced herself to smile instead of bursting into tears. "Thank you for your time, Mr. Seymour."

She walked out into the sunshine with her dignity more or less intact, but with absolutely no idea what to do next.

If she ever had the misfortune to set eyes on Edgar Whittemore again, she was going to wring his neck like that of a troublesome chicken—of the poultry variety, of course. They had never been friends, exactly, but she didn't remember ever treating him so horribly as to merit that kind of treatment.

She began to wander aimlessly down the sidewalk, moving only because people kept looking at her askance. She'd only gotten as far as the Mercantile—where she'd already been turned down by Tom Dunbarton despite his crisp white shirt— when a tall, willowy blonde girl dressed from jaw to heel in a frothy lemon concoction stepped into her path.

"Mrs. Carter?"

Was there any doubt? Eliza Jane couldn't imagine too many tall, black-haired unaccompanied women wandered around Gardiner. "Yes?"

"My name is Beth Ann Barnes." Even the soft, southern and utterly feminine drawl didn't keep Eliza Jane's skin from tightening up when she recognized the last name. The girl continued on, confirming her fears. "I'm Lucy Barnes's daughter."

Such a sweet, innocent appearing child had come from that fearsome shrew? Whatever the girl wanted, she apparently had no intention of moving until she'd said her piece. "What can I do for you, Miss Barnes?"

"Call me Beth Ann, please. And I need some advice about...a matter of the heart."

Eliza Jane managed to refrain from slapping herself in the forehead, but just barely. This couldn't be happening to her. "Beth Ann, I don't think—"

"My ma wants me to marry Sheriff Caldwell. Has her sights set on that something fierce. But I'm in love with Joey."

Eliza Jane mentally ran through the list of people she'd met, but came up empty. "Who is Joey?"

"Joey Keezer," Beth Ann answered in a loud whisper. "He rides for a ranch not far from here. But Ma says he's no kind of husband for a girl like me and that I'll marry the sheriff just as soon as she turns his mind to it."

Eliza Jane couldn't imagine this girl married to the dark and menacing sheriff. "I can't believe she wants to marry you off to that man."

A deceptively fragile-looking hand clutched Eliza Jane's forearm. "So you think I should run off with Joey?"

Oh, good Lord! "No, Beth Ann. You can't just run away to marry somebody your parents disapprove of."

"I'm old enough."

"Even so, running away is not the answer. Destroying your relationship with your family won't make you happy in the long run. You need to explain to your mother how you feel and keep on explaining until she has no choice but to listen."

Beth Ann's mouth drooped into a pretty pout. "Ma won't ever listen. And you're the one who goes around saying women should do whatever it is they feel like doing, whenever they want."

Eliza Jane jerked back as though she'd been slapped. "That is most certainly *not* the point of my lectures, young lady."

Her tone caused Beth Ann's eyes to widen and her jaw to drop, but Eliza Jane didn't care. There was a substantial difference between a woman having the right to make informed decisions about her own life and a young girl throwing her life away on a whim.

"You need to talk to your mother and tell her how you feel," she reiterated. "My lecture is mostly pointed toward married women and I absolutely do *not* recommend disobeying your mother or running away."

"But I love Joey," Beth Ann argued, and her sweet southern accent sounded a little less sweet.

"Then tell her that. Now, if you'll excuse me, I have some business to attend to."

The business she had been seeing to all day was an exercise in futility, of course, but it gave her an excuse to extricate herself from the awkward discussion.

As she neared the end of the main street, Eliza Jane considered paying a visit on the woman who had gazed at her so mournfully during her last lecture.

The woman's name, she had discovered from Marguerite, was Dandy Thayer, and she lived somewhere at that end of town. But Marguerite had warned her that, while Dandy vehemently denied he'd ever laid a hand on her, Roland Thayer was not a very nice man. He wouldn't take kindly to finding his wife in the company of a women's libber.

That only made Eliza Jane more determined to talk with Dandy. If what Marguerite said was true, Dandy had taken a risk in attending the lecture, and Eliza Jane considered that the woman was seeking a way to help herself.

But still, she wasn't willing to risk angering Roland Thayer by showing up unannounced on their doorstep with no knowledge of the man's schedule. She would simply keep an eye out for Dandy on the street and in the Mercantile, and maybe manage a private word with her.

For now Eliza Jane had to refocus her energies on finding employment. And from this point on she'd try to avoid proprietors in pink shirts.

৪০৪০০৪

"Hey, Doc. I'm heading over to the saloon for some lunch. Spare me a few minutes?"

Will wasn't much for the saloon, but he wouldn't be able to talk Adam into going anywhere else. If the sheriff didn't have his noonday shot of calm, there would be bodies by supper.

Maybe he'd even knock one back himself, just to cool the fire for a certain pain in the ass female that was burning in the pit of his stomach. But just the one.

When they stepped up to the bar, the barkeep set up the sheriff's glass, then looked Will over. "Howdy, Doc. I gotta warn you, we're fresh out of milk."

Will tried to stare him down, but the barkeep had too many years experience staring down badder men than Will Martinson. Finally, he gestured toward Adam's shot glass. "Give me what he's having."

"You sure, Doc? You remember what happened last time."

"*Hellfire*, just give me a drink. I only intend to have one."

The barkeep set him up a round and moved on down the counter. Since Adam was still too busy laughing at him to talk, Will perused the oil painting of a voluptuous nude hanging over the bar. As a rule he'd always found robust redheads mighty attractive, but now he'd bet Eliza Jane naked would make the artist's model look like a lump of unkneaded dough decked out in feathers and a red wig.

He took a sip off the whiskey, careful to keep his expression suitably manly while it seared a trail of fire down his gullet and exploded in his gut.

He'd just bet that, as tall as Eliza Jane was, her legs were plenty long enough to wrap around a man's waist and—

"We've got us a problem with that damn women's libber," Adam interrupted.

Of course, he didn't *know* he was interrupting. Or what. And since Will intended to keep it that way, he gave the sheriff his full attention. "What kind of problem?"

"Saw her talking to Beth Ann Barnes on the street a short time ago. That's a kind of trouble we don't need."

"Shit. I'll keep a closer eye on her." It was an appealing thought.

Adam polished off his drink and set the empty glass on the slab of polished wood hard enough to get the barkeep's attention. Will's was still three-quarters full, so he declined a second pour.

"The way I see it, Doc, it might be time for a little less watching and a little more action."

Will guessed when it came to Eliza Jane, the action he was considering taking and the action Adam was considering were mighty different. "What exactly is it you expect me to do, Sheriff? Lock her up 'til the stage comes through?"

He could tell by the silence the son of a gun was considering it. "Adam, she hasn't broken any laws. And trust me, she doesn't want to cross paths with Lucy Barnes any more than you do."

"Doubt that, since Lucy ain't looking to make *her* family."

They were quiet a moment, each lost in thought. Will's were a jumble and mostly centered around Eliza Jane—what she was doing, what she shouldn't be doing and what he *wanted* her to be doing.

"How's Miss Adele faring?" Adam asked after a while. Since Adam had as little as possible to do with the Chicken Coop, he was no doubt asking more for Will's sake than an overwhelming concern of his own.

"Not well," Will replied, staring down into the amber depths of his drink. "I don't reckon she'll hold out much longer."

It was a painful thing to contemplate, and he took a healthy swig of liquor. It burned, but not as badly as the thought of Miss Adele dying.

"I'll be sorry for her passing," Adam said, "on account of my knowing you think highly of her."

Will's glass was nearly empty, so he accepted more from the barkeep, then waited until the man moved on. "My own mother hasn't spoken to me since I volunteered as a Union doctor. I couldn't make my family understand why I thought preserving the country was so important. I write Ma a letter every year for her birthday, but she's never responded."

"I'm sorry for that, too, even though my brothers and I wore gray."

"You can quit being sorry for what you ain't done."

"It's an expression," the sheriff muttered. "And Miss Adele's an interesting choice to replace your ma."

"Nobody could replace my mother. But when I came to Gardiner and she approached me about tending to her chickens' medical needs, we just took a shine to one another."

"No offense, Doc, but I reckon she's taken a shine to a lot of fellows."

Will punched him in the arm. "Not that kind of shine. For me, Miss Adele is like a mother without the expectations and judgmental nature."

"Well, I tell you what. When she passes on, you and I can come here and I'll buy a bottle so you can have yourself a good cry."

The barkeep snickered and Will pushed away his glass. "You're such a good friend, Adam. But since everybody in Gardiner already knows I'm a maudlin drunk, if I take to the bottle to drown my sorrows, I reckon I'll do it in private."

"Don't feel bad, Doc," the barkeep interrupted. "You won't be the only man in this town sad to see that old whore go. We'll be raising our glasses to her when the time comes."

The Will Martinson he'd been before the war would have driven the man's teeth down his throat for referring to a woman Will cared about in such a disrespectful manner. But the years of horror, followed by his years of wandering and in Gardiner had mellowed him, and he knew no disrespect was intended. The man was a barkeep, Will was a doctor and Miss Adele was an old whore. Simple as that.

"That's real nice, but I'll do my heavy drinking alone, all the same."

"When the time comes I'll give you a bottle on the house. You can take it home with you."

Will nodded his appreciation and the man wandered off to serve a couple of cowboys who'd come in.

Adam stood and dropped a couple of coins on the bar. "Maybe you'll get drunk enough to do something about the hankerin' you've got for that damn women's libber."

Will didn't respond as he followed the sheriff out of the saloon into the blazing sun. He couldn't really deny he had a hunger for her, but he didn't want to talk about it, either.

Adam pushed back his hat to scratch his head. "Course, knowing her, she'll expect to be on top."

Before Will could think of a suitable reply—if there was one—the sheriff walked away, his laughter trailing behind him.

Chapter Six

It was with a weary soul and wearier feet Eliza Jane walked down the plank sidewalk to the Chicken Coop the following afternoon. Nobody in Gardiner was inclined to offer the troublesome women's libber a job, and their reactions had ranged from tear-inducing laughter to righteous indignation she had the gall to ask.

Even after Augustus divorced her, his settlement and her inheritance had more than met her financial needs. She'd never given more than a passing thought to money.

Now she was growing desperate. Despite what she'd told the sheriff, she had been keeping a small amount of cash on hand for incidental purchases when Edgar ran like the cowardly dog he was. If she was frugal, she could afford simple meals at the restaurant for a few more days. But if she didn't find a job, she would find herself in dire straits very soon.

She was still poor, still unemployed, and hoping like the dickens she was still early enough in the day to not catch the chickens plying their trade. There was only so much a woman could take in one day.

At the sound of the door closing, one of the chickens—a perky redhead named Betty—peered down over the stair railing with her hair tied up in rag curlers. "Howdy, Mrs. Carter!"

"Good afternoon, Betty. I've come to pay a call on Miss Adele, if it's a good time."

"We're all getting ready for work since our knittin's going a mite bit slower than we hoped, but Miss Adele just woke up from a nap and I reckon she'd be glad for the company. Go on back to her room if you like." She waved and went back to her preparations.

Miss Adele, even on her deathbed, managed to look more attractive than Eliza Jane felt. The madam waved a hand toward the gilt chair next to her bed. Folding her tall frame down onto the tiny, decorative seat made her feel even more gauche.

"My chickens tell me it's a beautiful day out there, Eliza Jane. Why the glum face?"

"Nobody will offer me a job," she replied, trying for a matter-of-fact tone, but even she could hear the despair in her voice.

"From what I hear, child, you've managed to make yourself mighty unpopular with both the menfolk *and* the Bible Brigade. Have you tried Marguerite over at the restaurant? She's a reasonable sort and always busy as a one-armed muleskinner."

"I'm not a very good cook, I'm afraid," Eliza Jane confessed. "I'm at wit's end, Miss Adele. I honestly am. That's why I came to you."

The woman's black-rimmed eyes widened. "You know I think the world of you, child. You even remind me a little bit of myself—raising hell and turning menfolk on their ear. But you ain't so much like me I think you'd make a good chicken."

Eliza Jane almost leapt off the chair when she realized how Miss Adele had taken her words. "No! No, I don't want to be a chicken. I mean, I like them just fine, but I... Well, to be honest, I'm not very good at *that*, either."

"Oh sweetheart, you just haven't met up with the right man yet."

Eliza Jane thought of Will and those naughty, delicious words he'd said to her behind his examination curtain. *...and the other hand is holding a pillow to her mouth so her screaming doesn't wake the whole damn town and she can't even talk because it's all she can do to breathe...* Lord, she felt the heat climb into her face just thinking about it.

Unfortunately, it seemed the madam didn't miss it. "I hear you've been keeping company with my William. Do you like him well enough?"

Well enough to *what*? She liked him well enough to be thinking about him at all hours. And she liked him well enough to practically drape herself across him in his exam room. "He's...nice."

"He's *nice*?"

"Yes. He's nice and he's smart and he's very handsome." Eliza Jane looked down at her hands. "To be honest, he makes me wish I was more like the chickens."

Miss Adele laughed until her dying lungs robbed her of air. "You don't have to be a whore to have sex with a man, child. You're even allowed to enjoy it."

Eliza Jane's face was so hot she was surprised her hair didn't catch fire. She couldn't believe she was having this conversation. And it certainly wasn't the topic she'd had in mind when she arrived.

Up until recently she would have found the idea of discussing her intimate matters with a prostitute preposterous, but now she found herself wishing she'd met this woman before she'd married Augustus.

"Eliza Jane, I know you consider yourself a liberated woman. Well, it's time to liberate yourself from feeling undue shame and go liberate that man from his clothes."

Her hand flew to her mouth, but not fast enough to catch the startled laughter. "Miss Adele, that's..."

"Scandalous? Child, I used to be a good girl—well, as good as I *could* be—but life became a whole lot more fun after I gave it up. You only get one chance, so it's up to you to decide if you want to go to your grave having lived what other people decided was a good life, or if you want to go out knowing you held on for one hell of a ride."

Eliza Jane's eyes inexplicably burned with tears despite her smile. "You make it sound so fun and easy."

"Oh, it can be fun, but it ain't always easy. And if you decide to bed William, I don't reckon you should advertise it. But sometimes you've just got to do what makes you happy and damn anybody who doesn't like it."

The madam was overtaken by another coughing fit, and though she was quick to discard her handkerchief, Eliza Jane saw the red stain on the white linen. She didn't need a Harvard medical degree to know Miss Adele was getting worse.

After sipping from the glass of water next to her bed, Miss Adele folded her hands under her ample breasts. "Since you've set your sights on bedding my William and not just any cowboy with jingling pockets, how is it you think I can help you?"

Despite Miss Adele's open and friendly manner, Eliza Jane found herself shifting nervously on the fragile seat. "I apologize for being forward and indelicate—"

The other woman interrupted her with a deep chuckle. "Not many folks would apologize for saying something indelicate to a whore."

"Miss Adele, regardless of your profession, I hold you in higher personal regard than some other women in this town."

The madam's expression made her feelings about Lucy Barnes and her followers quite plain. "Go back to the forward and indelicate thing you were about to say to me."

"Yes, about that. I was wondering if perhaps any of the business owners in town are particular...friends of yours."

Miss Adele's eyebrows rose into high, graceful arches. "That's quite a favor you're asking of me, Eliza Jane."

"I know. I'm sorry." Embarrassed, she got to her feet and considered how best to extricate herself from the conversation. She must be more tired and discouraged than she knew to ask a woman she barely knew to essentially blackmail a customer on her behalf. "I shouldn't have imposed on you like this."

Miss Adele grasped her wrist before she could flee the room. Though the grip was weak, Eliza Jane allowed herself to be stayed. "I can arrange for you to find a job, but I'll ask a mighty big favor in return."

"Anything." And she meant it. The idea of begging charity from any of the few friends she had in Gardiner was entirely unpalatable—even more unpalatable than extortion—and she'd do anything to avoid that.

"Nobody knows this, but I've sent a letter to my niece, Rebecca, asking her to come. If I die before she gets here, I want you to help my chickens. They may earn their livings being women, but in some ways they're like little girls, and ain't one of them with a lick of business sense. Without their mama figure, they might just fall to pieces."

Eliza Jane pulled back her arm until she was holding the other woman's hand. "I promise I'll tend to the chickens, Miss Adele. And you know Will won't let any harm come to them."

Miss Adele gave her a sly look. "Seems like you could watch over them *together*."

"You've got a unique way of matchmaking, Miss Adele. Will and I can discover our love for one another while playing father and mother to a coop of orphaned chickens?"

The madam winked. "It's a grand plan, ain't it?"

හ๛ผ

Will had heard all about Eliza Jane's futile search for employment. It seemed he couldn't walk two feet down the sidewalk before somebody stopped him with another gossipy chapter of the story. And too many people seemed to be enjoying it a little too much for his liking.

He knew he'd spent more time with her than most folks, but it still irked him they couldn't see she was a decent woman just trying to do what she thought was right.

Despite the late hour, a light still burned at the sheriff's office, so Will wandered over to see what was keeping Adam at work.

"Hey, Doc," Adam said when Will stepped in and closed the door behind him.

A young, battered-looking cowboy gazed mournfully at Will through the bars of his cell. "Howdy, Doc."

It took Will a moment to place him. The boy rode for one of the big neighboring spreads, and he'd treated him once for a busted leg he got breaking a particularly rowdy horse. Joey Keezer was his name.

"It's been a while since you found yourself in trouble, Joey. What did you do this time?"

"I done got assaulted by Mrs. Barnes is what I done! She pulled my ladder right over and damn near broke my neck. Then she started beating me in the head with that Bible of hers. That's a damn heavy book." He rubbed the back of his head to prove his point.

"Well, if it wasn't such a big book, she wouldn't have near as much to hold against people," Will reasoned. "What were you doing up on a ladder here in town?"

Adam chuckled and folded his arms over his chest, apparently content to let the prisoner do all the answering.

"I was...aiming to visit Beth Ann."

"With a ladder?"

Joey shrugged. "She was in her bedroom at the time, so it required a ladder."

Will shook his head. "Now, Joey, you know Mrs. Barnes has her sights set on Beth Ann marrying the sheriff here, so what possessed you to do a fool thing like that?"

"I ain't marrying nobody," Adam felt a need to put in. Will didn't have the heart to tell him that, according to the wagering, the majority of men in Gardiner thought differently.

"You're lucky Brent Barnes didn't skin you alive." Will debated on whether or not to help himself to Adam's coffee. He decided against it, because he planned to fall into bed within the next hour or so.

"He couldn't get to me, on account of his wife's arms flailing around, knocking me senseless with her Bible."

"What I want to know," Adam said, "is if Beth Ann was expecting you."

Red embarrassment crept up from the cowboy's neck to spread over his cheeks. "I ain't saying nothing that would compromise Beth Ann's reputation, Sheriff. Especially if Mrs. Barnes gets her way and you're going to end up as her husband."

"I guess that answers that," Will said. "I'd recommend you stick to the Chicken Coop for a while, Joey."

"I'm in love with her, Doc Martinson. I don't reckon the chickens can help me with that, and it would only make things worse with Beth Ann."

"Can't be any worse than sneaking into the girl's bedroom, especially if you ain't bright enough to wait until her parents have gone to bed."

"I was trying to convince her to run off with me, seeing as how her mama ain't never going to let her marry somebody like me."

"Even if you do convince that crazy bat to let you marry Beth Ann," Adam put in, "you should still run off. Having that woman for a mother-in-law would be the death of any man."

Will winked at Joey. "That's the God's-honest truth. So are you in here for committing a crime or for your own protection?"

"I don't rightly know anything but that Mrs. Barnes wanted the sheriff to shoot me and he said he'd see to me."

"Little bit of both," Adam added. "As long as he's locked up here I know he ain't getting in any more trouble and I don't have Mrs. Barnes after me. I'll send him back out to the ranch once the town's asleep and that should be the end of it."

"For now." Joey's expression took on a sullen cast. "Beth Ann and I aim to get married one way or another."

Adam shot the cowboy a stern look. "Unless either the one way or the other involves her parents' blessing, you'd best be prepared for some serious consequences."

"She's nineteen years old, Sheriff Caldwell. It ain't right they won't let her marry."

"Oh, they'll let her marry," Will said, "as long it's Adam she's marrying."

He laughed when the sheriff threw a crumpled up sheet of paper at him. "Don't you have some boils that needed lancing, Doc?"

"Nope, my doctorin's done for the day. Ain't got nothing better to do than keep you company."

He'd no sooner uttered the words than the door to the office opened and Dan O'Brien stepped in. "Sorry to intrude, Sheriff, but I been lookin' all over for the doc. You're needed at the hotel."

Will rubbed a hand over his face and nodded. That good night's sleep would have to wait. "I'll need to get my bag first. What's the problem?"

"I'm not sure, Doc. But Mrs. Carter asked me to fetch you to her."

"What's wrong with her?" He got right in the man's face. "Did somebody lay a hand on her?"

He knew there were some folks who didn't like having her around, but if some dumb son of a bitch had hurt her, they'd find out in a hurry he was as handy with a gun as he was with a stethoscope.

The man's Adam's apple bobbed and he shook his head. "I...I don't think so. She just told me she was feeling mighty poorly and asked me to send you to her room as soon as I could, unless you were with a patient."

Will brushed by him and practically ran down the sidewalk to get his medical bag. Eliza Jane hadn't looked ill at all last time he'd seen her, and she didn't seem the type to send for a doctor unnecessarily. So either something had come upon her in a hurry, or somebody had decided to teach the women's libber a lesson.

If that was the case, there would be hell to pay.

Chapter Seven

Eliza Jane sat on the edge of her bed, waiting anxiously for the doctor to arrive. She was as nervous about the false pretenses as she was about the reason for them, and she only hoped Will wouldn't be too upset with her.

When the knock sounded on her door, she jumped to her feet. "Who is it?"

"Mrs. Carter, it's Doctor Martinson. Mr. O'Brien said you were feeling poorly."

He sounded so...formal. Was somebody listening? Or was he annoyed at being called to her room at such a late hour? "Come in."

Will opened the door and stepped in, blinking in the dim light before closing the door behind him. His eyes widened when he saw her, standing there in nothing but her silk wrapper and scandalously bare feet. She was freshly bathed, and she'd brushed her hair until it shone like onyx before sending the note down with the part-time kitchen girl who'd been passing by her room.

"You look mighty healthy for a sick woman," he said after a moment.

"I...I'm not really sick." She felt the flush across her chest and up onto her neck at her admission. "In order to send for you, I either needed a doctor or a lawman, and if I'd only asked for a lawman, I might have ended up with Sheriff Caldwell, and...well, that wouldn't have done at all."

She took heart when Will bolted the door. Surely he wasn't in the habit of locking himself in the room with his patients. "So if you're not sick and you haven't committed a crime, what is it I can do for you, Eliza Jane?"

She felt incredibly vulnerable and foolish, but she'd come too far to turn back now. Even if she tried to send him away, Will wasn't going to leave without an explanation. "I've been having a rough time of things lately, as you know, and I've decided to reach and grab some happiness for myself. I want to...I want you to..."

She looked at him beseechingly, but he crossed his arms and shook his head. "Oh, I'm going to make you say it, darlin'."

Eliza Jane sucked in a deep breath, then just blurted it out. "I want you to make love to me."

His cocky smile faded, but the desire in his eyes was hot enough to curl her hair. "Darlin', I ain't in the habit of taking advantage of a woman who's feeling low."

He didn't know her very well if he thought she was going to be deterred that easily now that she'd committed herself. "You listen to me, Will Martinson. I was a good and dutiful wife and that got me nothing. I've been a staunch advocate for women and I have nothing again. Now it's time to be an advocate for myself. It's time for me to do something just for myself."

Eliza Jane didn't look away while Will seemed to search her face for something—maybe a sign she wasn't just looking for easy comfort she'd regret in the morning.

"I'm sure," she said, hoping to help him along since it was rather awkward standing there, offering herself to him. "I want this itch scratched and only you can do it."

He didn't laugh as she'd expected, or even crack a smile. "How sure are you, darlin'? Because once I start touching you, I ain't gonna want to stop. I will if you ask me, but then I'd have to turn you over to Adam for minding."

"I don't need minding," she felt compelled to protest. "And I've never been more sure of anything."

She held her breath, wondering how she'd endure the humiliation should Will reject her. She had been so sure he desired her physically, but now that she was practically throwing herself at him, she couldn't help but wonder if she'd misjudged him. Or maybe he'd be put off by her forwardness.

"Do...do you want me?"

The smoldering look in his eyes gave depth to the easy grin. "Darlin', I want you so much I'm likely to look like a fool if I don't take a moment to compose myself."

Maybe it was silly to get such a thrill from her effect on him, but she couldn't help herself. And his candidness made her feel bold. "I've been waiting a long while for you to scratch this itch, Will Martinson."

Without taking his eyes from her, Will took off his hat and tossed it onto the armchair. Her hands went to the sash of her robe, but he shook his head while taking tauntingly slow steps toward her.

"I'm going to unwrap you myself, darlin'," he said, as if she were a gift to be savored.

Just the way Will looked at her took Eliza Jane's breath away. She was trembling, and she wondered at her sense of anticipation. She wasn't a virgin, after all. She had some idea of what to expect.

Any second Will would lower her to the mattress, part her robe and take his pleasure. Then he would either roll over and go to sleep or return to his own bed, leaving her with a tiny ache at the small of her back and the certainty there should have been more.

...your husband wasn't doing it right.

He tugged at the sash, pulling her close to him. "So if this itch of yours is that bad, I reckon I'd better give you a thorough examination. Where do you think I should start?"

She had to swallow hard before she could answer. Being wanton wasn't a usual part of her nature, or so she'd thought. "I don't know, Doctor. I itch all over."

"I'll start at the top, then."

And he did. Will let go of her sash and threaded his fingers through her hair, pulling her into his kiss. When his lips touched hers, Eliza Jane couldn't hold back the sigh. The last of her anxiety over her scandalous behavior faded away and she melted into his embrace.

He kissed her thoroughly, his tongue dancing over hers, until her toes were curled against the hardwood floor and his shirt was bunched in her fists.

Will's mouth left hers and began blazing a hot, moist trail down her neck, until Eliza Jane could barely breathe, never mind speak. His hands ran over her shoulders, and he cupped their roundness, squeezing gently. His thumbs skimmed over her collarbones, as his lips pressed to the hollow between them, and she threw back her head, baring her throat to his kiss.

"You smell mighty pretty, Eliza Jane," he said against her skin. Then he licked that small hollow. "You taste good, too."

Being brazen was going well for her so far, so she ran her hands over his chest to his top button and started working her way down.

Engrossed as she was in liberating him from his shirt, the warm whisper of air over her own naked skin came as a surprise. She hadn't even been aware of Will pulling free the loose knot of her sash until he slid the robe from her shoulders.

Shyness overcame her as she stood nude before him, despite the low appreciative growl that came deep from his throat. The urge to cross her arms over her breasts—to somehow cover herself—was strong, until Will bent and drew one erect nipple into the moist heat of his mouth. He ran his tongue over the sensitive bud, and that was the last she thought of being shy.

Somehow Will managed to caress and kiss what seemed like every part of her body while divesting himself of his clothing.

He ran his hands down her back from her neck to her hips, molding her body to his. Because Eliza Jane was taller than average, she was a perfect fit, and at that moment she would have been content to stand there forever, soaking in his warmth.

Until Will reached down, gripped her buttocks and lifted her as he bent his knees, drawing the long, hard length of him against the juncture of her thighs. Eliza Jane gasped and grabbed onto his shoulders in case her trembling knees gave out.

"You know, darlin'," he said in a low voice as he backed her toward the bed, "if you take to screaming too loud, people will wonder exactly what kind of medical treatment it is I'm giving you."

"I'll try to remember to scream into the pillow," she promised.

When she found herself on her back on the bed with Will standing over her, Eliza Jane let her gaze roam boldly over his body. He was all hard planes and lean muscle, with a sprinkling of hair across his chest that tapered down toward...

Oh my. No wonder he had a little swagger in his walk, if his stride had to accommodate that. And though—as she'd told him—she wasn't ignorant of the act, she had some doubts about her body's ability to welcome a manhood of such impressive stature.

Will tucked his knees between hers, took her hands and stretched her arms up over her head as he lowered his body. She arched her back to meet him halfway.

He grinned. "Are you a wanton woman, Eliza Jane?"

She froze, unsure of what he wanted the answer to be. His expression implied he was enjoying her brazen behavior, but you never could tell with a man.

"I think you are," he continued in a low, husky voice that made her shiver. He pressed his erection against her lower abdomen and circled his hips, grinding himself against her until she whimpered, wanting more. "And I think you're going to ruin me for any other woman."

Because she didn't want to consider Will doing this with any other woman, she nodded. He laughed, then bent his head to nip at her ear.

Will managed to work his mouth down to her breasts while still making those lazy circles of his hips against hers. She wrapped her legs around his waist trying to urge him downward, but he didn't budge. She tried to pull her hands free so she could help things along, but he wouldn't release her.

"Tell me what you want, darlin'."

Eliza Jane felt the heat of a blush spread across her chest and face. Surely he didn't expect her to speak a thought like that out loud.

But apparently he did. "I've not known you to have a problem speaking your mind yet, Eliza Jane, so don't be shy with me now."

She looked into his clear blue eyes and took a deep breath. "I want to feel you inside of me."

He kissed her, devouring her mouth as he reached down between their bodies and guided himself into her.

Eliza Jane sighed against his lips as he filled her slowly—gently easing forward, pulling back, then easing a little more until her body had taken all of him. She gripped the brass rails of the headboard, instinctively raising her hips to meet each thrust.

He looked down at her, watching her face intently. She gave him a naughty grin of her own. "I think I *am* a wanton woman, after all. I do believe you're a bad influence on me, Doctor Martinson."

"Darlin', I aim to influence you 'til you beg for mercy."

There was a fine sheen of sweat glistening on his forehead, and she noticed the trembling in his shoulders as he held his weight off of her. His thrusts were quickening, deepening, and her body was urging him on, aching for...something.

"I never beg," Eliza Jane said breathlessly.

She gasped when Will drove into her, a small cry escaping her lips. He curled his hands over hers as she held the headboard and used his arms to pull his body forward, burying himself in her over and over until she was sobbing his name.

Their breaths came fast and shallow, and she moaned, locking her ankles together over his hips.

"Tell me how it feels, darlin'," he demanded in a harsh whisper.

She couldn't even think, never mind finding the words to describe how she felt. Never in her life had she experienced the sensations taking over her body. "It feels so...right."

Will released her hands so he could slide his own under her, cupping her head and lifting her face to his. Their panting breaths mingled as he drove deep within her. Then she succumbed to a pleasure she'd never felt before while Will muffled her screams with his kiss. As her body trembled, she heard him moan her name and felt his hot seed fill her.

He pressed short, sweet kisses to her hairline, her cheeks, the tip of her nose, while tremors shook his body.

Eliza Jane pried her fingers from the brass rails and ran her hands down Will's sweat-slickened back. "Oh...*my*."

He chuckled and rested his head on her chest. "I agree."

Now she knew why the occasional woman would outright laugh when Eliza Jane suggested forgoing intimacy for part of each month. What woman in her right mind would pass up a chance to feel like *this*?

And Will was right. Augustus hadn't been doing it right at all.

"You're awfully quiet," Will mumbled against her breast. "When you go too long without talking, I start getting nervous."

She lazily stroked his hair, liking the way it made him shiver. "I'm simply enjoying the moment."

"Simply enjoy it for a few more moments, darlin', and then we're going to do it all over again. I ain't nearly had my fill of you yet."

"Oh my."

৪০৪০৫

Will yawned—again—and hoped he wouldn't fall asleep face-down in his eggs. Adam would never let him live that down.

As it was, he was glad they were regular customers because he was too damn tired to even read a menu.

Not that he was complaining any. He'd just passed the best and most pleasurable night of his life exploring Eliza Jane and if waking up with yolk on his nose and bacon grease in his hair was the price he'd pay, it would be well worth the cost.

"So, how's that women's libber of yours?" Adam asked. "Sounded like she was feeling poorly last night."

Will took a swig of coffee trying to wake himself up. "She's feeling better."

"Cured her of what ails her, did you?" Adam had a gleam in his dark eyes that told Will not to bother trying to fool him for a second.

"I don't give information on my patients," he said. "And I expect the sheriff to show the same discretion, as well."

Adam snorted. "Hell, the last thing I need is for Lucy Barnes to have another reason to whack me with that Bible of hers."

Will stabbed his fork into his eggs, but didn't raise it to his mouth. "I don't know what to do about Eliza Jane."

The sheriff had no such problems with his appetite, but at least he had the good grace to swallow before saying, "You should have just let me shoot her right off. Now it's too late because I figure it's wrong to shoot your friend's woman."

"Probably." Will swallowed down more coffee, pondering what the hell he was supposed to do about the woman.

It turned out she wasn't one of those itches a man could scratch once and be done with. Wanting her was a persistent itch he could feel growing under his skin again already, even as exhausted as he was.

"Don't moon over the girl while I'm eating," Adam said. "You'll give me a sour stomach."

"I'm not mooning. I'm considering."

"Considering what?" Adam waved his fork at him. "You know what you should do? You should marry her."

Well if that just wasn't the most damn fool thing he'd ever heard. Mostly. "I never pegged you as a man who'd preach wedded bliss, Adam."

"Oh hell, not for me. And I doubt there'd be much *bliss* for the man married to that woman."

Oh, if he only knew. Bliss didn't even begin to describe what Eliza Jane made him feel. Of course, there was a lot more to marriage than lovemaking, but it was one hell of a good start.

"But," Adam continued, "it would go a long way toward appeasing the Bible Brigade."

"I ain't swearing 'til death do us part to a woman so Lucy Barnes will stop pestering you about her. And you know you aren't getting a lick of peace from that woman until you marry her daughter, anyway."

"You're changing the subject."

"You're the one who brought up marriage."

"For you and that women's libber." Adam pushed his empty plate to the side and reached across the table for Will's untouched plate. He let it go without a fight, but snagged the sheriff's almost full coffee cup. "What's she going to do now?"

"Keep hunting for a job, I reckon."

"Ain't nobody gonna hire her, Doc. Best thing that woman can do is borrow the traveling money she needs to go home."

Will only shrugged, but privately he didn't think that was at all the best thing for Eliza Jane.

Eliza Jane stood at the window of her hotel room, watching Will and the sheriff leave the restaurant. She couldn't hold back the girlish smile that bloomed when Will looked up at her window. She didn't think he could see her through the lacy curtain, but she got a little thrill from the fact he'd looked up. That meant he was thinking about her.

The two men stood talking for a few minutes. Even though there had been a note from Miss Adele under her door when she woke telling her to report to the dressmaker's shop at ten o'clock, she let herself linger.

They were both incredibly handsome men, but Adam Caldwell didn't cause her stomach to somersault the way looking at Will did. She felt like a silly young girl again as she watched the man who'd treated her as anything but the night before talk to his friend.

Then they went their separate ways, but not before Will looked up at her window again. This time, though, he grinned and tipped his hat, and she knew she'd been caught.

She laughed and turned away from the window to prepare for the day. Maybe being stranded in Gardiner a little longer wasn't such a bad thing after all.

Chapter Eight

Four days later, Will leaned against the outside of the Mercantile, sucking on a piece of penny candy and watching Eliza Jane drag a bale of hay across the livery corral. Adam also held up a section of wall, sucking another piece of candy he'd filched from Will's bag.

Will had to admit Eliza Jane had gumption. It was hard, hot work for anybody, least of all a woman. But she was slowly getting the bale to the trough where the horses stood waiting. Adam's ugly-as-sin gelding stood slightly apart, watching the woman with an impatient, grumpy expression that matched his owner's.

Will's patience finally paid off when Eliza Jane paused once again to stretch. She placed her hands on the small of her back and arched her body, which caused her breasts to thrust forward in a most attractive manner.

"You better not be looking at her bosom," he muttered to Adam.

"Doc, you and I been friends a long time, but you can bet your ass I'm looking at that bosom. You're a lucky man."

He thought so, too. "She shouldn't be working at the livery stable. It's no job for a woman."

"What I want to know is *how* she got the job in the first place. Last I heard Johnny Barnes had threatened to steal my thunder and shoot her before I could. And even though old man Digger still owns the place, Johnny pretty much runs it."

Will reached into his bag for another piece of candy. If he and Adam stood around much longer there'd be none left for his young patients. "Eliza Jane had a private talk with Melinda and she went on home to her family. And don't tell nobody, but Miss Adele's called in a few favors on her behalf."

Eliza Jane went back to dragging the hay bale, much to their disappointment.

"It doesn't surprise me none that madam of yours would cotton to a women's libber," Adam said. "But what the hell kind of favor could the dressmaker owe a whore?"

Will shrugged. Eliza Jane had lasted less than a day working for the dressmaker. After she'd miscut a yard of overpriced fabric, and managed to stick herself and bleed all over a length of tacked lace, the dressmaker's wife herself had sent a note to Miss Adele and told her she already knew the secret the madam was holding over her husband's head and the women's libber was done making dresses.

She'd gone through a few other businesses as well before winding up at the livery stable, doing a man's job.

Eliza Jane stretched again, and again conversation lagged while they watched her. She was going to be sore as hell come the end of the day. Will supposed, as the town's doctor, it was his sworn duty to massage those aching muscles for her.

While in her bed.

Naked.

"You need to put a stop to this," Adam declared, jerking him out of his thoughts of impending medical treatment.

"I tried my damndest to talk her out of it this morning, but she's determined to set an example for the women in this town. Wants to prove she can fend for herself in a man's world. If I interfere, she'll hate me for it."

"How much money you reckon that Whittemore fellow took off with? I could ride out of here for a while, then ride back in and tell her I got her money back."

Will shifted his weight back and forth on his feet, feeling like a yellow-bellied snake. "I considered that, but we don't know how much he took. Plus, if we did that, she'd have all the money she needed."

The sheriff slanted him a sideways look. "She'd have enough to hightail it out of here, you mean."

Hellfire. "I don't want to watch her breaking her back for short pay, but I don't want her to get on the next stage out of here, either."

Adam held out his hand for another piece of penny candy. "She'll either stay here for you or she won't, Doc."

"I just need a little more time."

Would there ever be enough time? A woman like Eliza Jane might never be happy in a place like Gardiner. And what the hell did he have to offer her but what she'd devoted her life to fighting against?

And he was trying his damndest to be sensible, too. The fact she managed to tie him into knots and made him feel about ten feet tall in bed didn't mean he was feeling the kind of love that would make him want Eliza Jane forever. But he certainly did want her right now.

"I tried to talk her into working for me," Will said to fill the silence. "But she knows my money's old family money, not pay for doctoring, and she figures I only told her I needed an assistant to hide my charitable intentions."

"Did she try Marguerite over at the restaurant?"

"Seems she doesn't cook any better than she sews."

Adam snorted. "How the hell did she ever get herself a husband?"

"Financial arrangement between her father and him, I reckon. It sure as hell wasn't her domestic skills." The man hadn't deserved her, though, no matter how he'd gotten her. "I'd wager the man already had an army of servants."

"Why didn't that madam of yours find her a place at the Coop?"

Will almost choked on his penny candy. "Like *hell*."

"Not on her back, jackass. Like as a housekeeper or the person who keeps all that frilly stuff they wear washed."

"Working in a whorehouse—in *any* capacity—isn't for a woman like Eliza Jane."

Adam waved a hand at her as she tried to hoist the bale into the trough. "And that is? Why don't you just marry her and be done with it?"

"She's like a skittish, unbroken filly. You can't start out by just throwing a saddle on her and expect her not to buck you off."

Adam grunted. "You'd be better off just getting yourself a nice, docile mare already broke to the bit."

Will was mighty glad Eliza Jane couldn't hear them comparing women to horses or she'd have slapped both their faces. But the truth was, he didn't *know* what he wanted. Who was to say he and a woman like Eliza Jane could make a life together? About the only thing he *did* know was that he didn't want her skedaddling out of town before they even had a chance to find out.

Finally, she cut the twine and the bale of hay collapsed into the trough. Her face was red with exertion and sweat glimmered on her skin, but she smiled when she finally noticed him watching. The sleeves of her white blouse were folded to her elbows and she wiped her forehead with the back of her arm before giving him a wave. The she clapped her leather-clad hands together and started back toward the stable.

Well, hell. She looked pretty damn proud of herself. Sure, she'd be a hurting lady later, but right now even a blind man couldn't miss the glow of satisfaction under all that sweat.

"If I interfere with her doing her job," he said to Adam, "it's as good as saying I have no respect for her. Considering she already has a fairly low opinion of men in general, I reckon she wouldn't take too kindly to that."

"Well, if she's going to be doing this every day, we're going to need more penny candy."

৪৩৪০৫৪

Eliza Jane had made a point of telling everybody she saw the sheriff's horse had stepped on her foot and the pain had grown to be almost more than she could bear. She'd even practiced her fake limp, taking special care to always favor the same foot.

Only when she was confident she'd given enough people a logical explanation for her visiting the doctor after dark did she step into Will's office. They locked the door, left the office lit and crept up the back stairs to make love in his bed by the moonlight.

Their lovemaking was an experience that took her breath away. He liked to explore her body, all the while watching her closely to judge what she liked best.

She liked it all. Will had deft fingers which easily found just the right spots to make her sigh or squirm or even scream into his pillow. He liked to run his fingers though her hair and then tickle her breasts with the strands. She didn't think there was an inch of her body he hadn't touched and stroked, even tasted.

Not that she didn't do her share of exploring, as well. She'd discovered his nipples were as sensitive as her own, and that he absolutely hated having his feet touched. Using her teeth to nip at his earlobes drove him wild to the point his hips would lift off the bed, and kisses to the small of his back always made him moan.

Tonight he'd offered to knead her sore muscles, and he had—before moving on to muscles that weren't really even sore at all. Now she was sprawled naked on her back, but she lifted her head to look down at Will.

"I love this little freckle right here," he said, pressing a kiss to the inside of her thigh. Then his lips moved a little higher. "And this one."

Eliza Jane laughed and tried to pull her leg away. "I only have *one* there."

He held tight, and his next kiss made her suck in a breath. "Hush. I'm using my imagination."

It was a while before she could think straight again, and at that point she was panting and covered in a fine sheen of sweat.

"Oh my," she whispered.

He kissed her stomach before moving his body up hers. "You are such a wanton woman," he told her just as the full length of him slid easily inside of her.

Eliza Jane arched her back, her arms looping around his neck. "That's your fault, you know. I didn't use to be."

He raised himself onto his forearms so he could look down into her face. She knew he liked to watch her when the pleasure overtook her, even if she closed her eyes.

"No, darlin'. You've always been a passionate woman. I was just the lucky man who discovered it."

But as his thrusts quickened and her eyes slid closed, she knew he was wrong. Will hadn't discovered her passion. He'd awakened it, and she gave it all to him now, losing herself in him as he took them over the edge together.

After a few minutes, with her work-sore muscles soothed by his touch and the languid aftermath of pleasure, she snuggled into his embrace. "Tell me how a doctor from the finest medical school in the country ended up in a town like this."

"Believe it or not, darlin', I come from a long line of rich doctors. After Harvard, I had myself a private practice treating the cream of Virginia society. Then war was declared. Between volunteering to do my part and, in the eyes of most, volunteering for the wrong side, I gave that up."

"I'm sure your fellow Virginians weren't very forgiving after the war ended."

"It wouldn't have mattered. I came out of the Union hospital tents tired of blood and suffering. I wandered out west—broke horses, tended bar, whatever came along. One day I drifted into Gardiner and found scarlet fever. I dusted off my bag and never got around to leaving."

It wasn't quite as simple as that. She could hear it in his voice. "You actually *like* it here, don't you?"

"This is home, darlin', and these are good people. They ain't all quite right in the head, and Adam and Lucy are downright scary at times, but they're good people." He yawned and pulled her even closer.

This was where sneaking around became problematic. He wanted to hold her close and go to sleep. But, while she liked the holding close part, she couldn't stay. So she kept talking.

"You don't sound like a man with a degree from Harvard Medical School, you know. You sound like you were born and raised here in Gardiner."

He gave a little laugh. ""I'm a southern boy by birth anyway, so it didn't take long for all that proper grammar to fade away. And folks are more comfortable talking to somebody who sounds like them."

"So you did it on purpose?"

"For a while. Now it's just who I am."

Eliza Jane propped herself up on her elbow so she could gaze down at him. "I like who you are."

"It suits me." He reached up to play with a strand of her hair. "*You* suit me."

"I suit you in bed." She planted a light kiss on his mouth. "I suit you far less when I'm fully clothed."

When he didn't answer right away, Eliza Jane got a sinking feeling in the pit of her stomach. She knew he enjoyed her body far more than her mind but, despite her teasing, she didn't want him to admit it out loud.

"You do cause a mite bit more trouble with your clothes on," Will finally said, "but if it was only a matter of being naked, a quick trip to the Chicken Coop would be a sight easier than sneaking around with you, darlin'."

That was sweet in a roundabout sort of way, so she kissed him again. Then, despite knowing it wasn't the best time or place for it, she asked the question that had been on her mind a lot lately. "Why aren't you married, Will?"

"That sure would make our current relationship a lot more complicated, now wouldn't it?"

"I'm serious." She rested her head on his chest again. "Have you ever *had* a wife?"

"Nope. It takes a special kind of woman to be a doctor's wife, and I guess I never found her."

She knew she shouldn't ask, but then again, she shouldn't be lying naked in the man's bed, either. "How is a doctor's wife special?"

"Well, a doctor doesn't work set hours. His wife has to be willing to make him a hot supper at two in the morning if that's when he's finished with a child birthing or nursing an ill patient. Sometimes the laundry ain't especially pretty, and the office and the exam room have to be kept very clean. And more than one doctor's had to leave a Christmas celebration to tend to somebody. And his wife has to be willing to bear all that without complaint."

"I guess I'm the opposite of everything a doctor's wife has to be."

He was silent for a few seconds, then he said quietly, "Yeah, you are, darlin'."

It shouldn't have bothered her to hear it. She'd asked nothing of Will, after all, and he'd made her no promises. She didn't even *want* those kinds of promises, having had them broken so painfully before. It still made her ache just a little, though, knowing deep down she didn't suit him all that well after all.

"But then again," Will continued, "a doctor ain't usually a lawman, either, so neither one of us is typical."

Eliza Jane was too tired to wade any further into this conversational quagmire, so she trailed her fingernails down over his chest...and lower. "Hmm...if you're not a typical doctor, maybe that's why this itch you're treating for me keeps coming back."

Will growled and rolled so he was looking down at her. He didn't look quite so sleepy now. "Let's give it a really good scratching, darlin'."

80&0C3

It was another three days before Eliza Jane got ahead enough in her work at the livery to pay a late morning visit to the Chicken Coop. She wanted to check on Miss Adele and Sadie in particular, but the others as well.

The chicken strike hadn't lasted very long. The girls needed to earn money and the men had been pretty persistent in their arguments against the knitting. Texas cowboys apparently didn't feel much of a need for mismatched knitted socks with crooked heels and bunched toes. They *did* feel the need for their randier pursuits.

The house was quiet when she entered, but she spotted Sadie right away, tucked into a chair in the corner of the parlor and knitting what appeared to be a blanket. Eliza Jane walked over and sat near her on the settee. Sadie was counting stitches, so she waited until she reached the end of the row before saying good morning.

"Good morning, Mrs. Carter." She held up her knitting. "What do you think?"

"I think you're getting much better at it," Eliza Jane said diplomatically. Despite the amount of time she spent counting, Sadie's rows never all had the same number of stitches. "I haven't seen you in a while, so I thought I'd stop and see how you're doing."

"I feel a little poorly when I first wake up, but Doc says that's okay. Otherwise I'm fine."

"Have you given any more thought to your future? To the baby's future?"

Sadie's mouth flattened into a stubborn line Eliza Jane didn't find at all encouraging. "I reckon I'll keep doing what I've always done and just make do the best I can for the baby."

"You can't raise your child at the Chicken Coop, Sadie."

"Why not? It wouldn't be the first young'un running around a whorehouse, you know. And we're a family—the only family I got. I know Miss Adele won't toss us out."

She hadn't come with the intention of lecturing Sadie, but now she couldn't help herself. "But what kind of life will that be for the child? He or she won't be treated kindly. And if that baby should grow to have an unmistakable likeness to the father, you could have all sorts of trouble."

Sadie drew in a deep breath, using it to heave a mighty sigh. "I don't know no life but whoring, Mrs. Carter. I ain't never going back to the place I came from, and even if I moved on to another town, whoring's all I can do. At least here I know Miss Adele's gonna take care of us."

Eliza Jane wasn't certain the madam would even live to see the baby, never mind help raise it, but she didn't have the heart to say it aloud.

"Isn't there anything else at all you're skilled at?" she asked.

Sadie thought about it for a minute. "No, Mrs. Carter. Makin' men feel good is about all I know how to do."

Now it was Eliza Jane who sighed. "What if I could find a good home for your baby, Sadie. Maybe a couple who can't have children of their own."

"I ain't giving my baby to no strangers to raise. I already love her...or him. I even quit the whorin' part 'til after the baby comes. Miss Adele told me I could cook and clean and do some mending to earn my keep for now."

There wasn't anything more Eliza Jane could do to change her mind right then, and she didn't want to push too hard. She wanted Sadie to be comfortable talking to her. "It's good that you've stopped taking customers. And speaking of Miss Adele, I think I'll go see if she's up to a visit."

The madam was awake and—as always—looking her best, all things considered. "I was hoping you'd stop by soon, Eliza Jane. I've missed your company."

"I've been busy during the day at the livery, and in the evening... Well, that's not a convenient time to visit the Coop, of course. But I wanted to thank you for helping me find work."

Miss Adele waved away her gratitude. "You look immeasurably more cheerful today, child. Come to think of it, my William's been mighty cheerful of late, as well. I do believe I heard him whistling when he left here this morning."

"Yes, well..." Eliza Jane blushed, but stopped trying to hold back the grin. "The past few days have been very liberating."

"Good for you, child. I knew you two were a good match."

The smile froze on Eliza Jane's face. "We're not *that* kind of match, Miss Adele. We're just...being liberated together for a while."

The other woman barely had the air to laugh anymore, but she managed a small one anyway. "I know a good match when I see one. You and that boy will be liberatin' one another for a good long time."

Sadness had Eliza Jane looking down at her hands. "I know you care for Will a great deal, and it's natural to look to your loved ones' futures when you're ailing, but that's not going to happen. I can't stay here."

"Why not?"

"Well, half the town wants to string me up, for one thing. The sheriff alternates between laughing at me and threatening to shoot me. My real work is women's suffrage, not lugging hay for smelly horses—not that I don't appreciate the job. And I never intended to stay this long."

"I think that fellow running off with your money is the best thing that ever happened to you and you just don't know it yet."

Eliza Jane hadn't come to spend the day arguing with a dying woman, so she only sighed and shook her head. Whether

Miss Adele chose to believe it or not, Gardiner was just one stop on her path, even if it was a longer stop than most.

"You're happy with my William now, child. What makes you think you wouldn't be in the future?"

"Because he needs a dutiful, domestic doctor's wife, and I'm not that. I can't ever be that."

"I know that boy, and he's not the kind to stifle a woman or try to change her ways."

"With all due respect, he's never had any legal authority over you. Since he's never been married, nobody can actually say what kind of husband he'd be. And I can't change who I am to make him happy."

Miss Adele reached out and took her hand. "Child, I guess you just don't know who you really are yet."

Chapter Nine

Tormenting his feisty women's libber grew to be Will's favorite pastime over the next several days, even if he did wind up torturing himself damn near as much as he did Eliza Jane.

If he passed her on the sidewalk, he'd brush up against her. He'd give her what he hoped were sultry glances when nobody else was looking. At the Mercantile, when Tom had his back turned, he'd stepped up behind her at the counter so close he could feel the heat of her warming his body. And every morning he and Adam went through their body weight in penny candy watching her bring hay to the horses.

It was a game meant to keep Eliza Jane constantly aware of him—constantly wanting him. The unfortunate side effect was Will going about his days in an almost constant state of arousal. If he didn't come up with a good excuse for being alone with her damn soon, he was likely to give her something a sight more scandalous than a spanking right in the middle of the street.

A plan had started to form involving a note, a map and a picnic blanket when the door to his office opened.

Hellfire. It wasn't her. Instead, Johnny Barnes stuck his head in.

"Hey, Doc. You busy?"

He didn't intend to share how he'd been musing about the freckle on the inside of Eliza Jane's left thigh, so he shook his head. "What can I do for you, Johnny?"

Since the man's face and neck were a flaming crimson, he either had one of the worst fevers Will had ever seen or he was suffering from a mighty personal problem. And seeing as how Johnny was up on his feet, he assumed it was the latter.

"That Mrs. Carter, she's been talking to Melinda now and again about...women stuff."

Will nodded, trying to hide his mixed reaction. On the one hand, his libido had perked right up at the mention of Eliza Jane. On the other, his mind knew her name coming into a conversation usually spelled trouble.

Johnny took a seat, seemingly just wanting a place to squirm. "Well, Melinda and me, we done some talking, too, and it's a fine idea to wait until Johnny Junior's a might bit older before we have another young'un."

"That not a bad idea at all. Melinda's a young, pretty girl and there's no sense in wearing her out having one baby after another. You've got plenty of time for more children."

"Right. So we're not going to...that is, we'll keep track of her...um...so there's time..."

"You're going to avoid making love during the days of her cycle she's more likely to conceive?"

Johnny's relief came out in a rush of air. "That's it exactly, Doc."

Will leaned back in his chair. "If you're looking for me to tell you Mrs. Carter's methods will guarantee you don't have a baby, I can't do that. All it does is give you better odds."

"Mrs. Carter did explain all that to Melinda—how it's not for certain. That's...not really why I came to see you."

The way the young man was squirming again, Will was beginning to wonder if he was really suffering from some kind of posterior rash.

"Melinda said Mrs. Carter told her if I got too randy during those times I should...just take my own self in hand—and that's not any way for womenfolk to be talking if you ask me."

But Will didn't ask him because *randy, Mrs. Carter* and *taken in hand* had all jumbled together to make one hell of a picture in his mind.

"But the thing is, my ma," Johnny continued, and the mention of Lucy Barnes snapped Will right back to the here and now. "She used to tell me when I was a young'un that real bad things would happen to me if I...took myself in hand."

Only years of doctorly discipline and the look on Johnny's face kept Will from laughing—or even cracking a smile. But there wasn't enough discipline in the world to keep from asking, "What kind of real bad things?"

Johnny looked down at his feet, which he kept shuffling around. "Mostly she didn't really say what, but one time she told me touching myself there caused a sickness that would make my prick wither up and fall off."

"Damn, Johnny, that must have made it scary to take a piss."

He gave the man a moment to catch up to the conversation, and then almost *did* laugh when his mouth dropped open. "Are you tellin' me my ma wasn't entirely truthful?"

Will hadn't gotten a medical degree by being stupid enough to call Lucy Barnes a liar outright. And yet he couldn't let the poor kid go on thinking he'd be gelded if he got a little frisky with himself. "Don't you reckon if a man touching his prick too much made it fall off, you'd see a lot more men sitting down to piss?"

Johnny gave him a sheepish shrug. "I thought maybe Mrs. Carter suggested it so as to make men's peckers fall off on account of her not liking them and all."

Will wasn't sure if Johnny was implying Eliza Jane didn't like men or didn't like peckers, but he wasn't inclined to set the boy straight about how wrong he was on the latter. The former, however, was still a little up in the air.

"Mrs. Carter's a pretty smart lady, Johnny, and all she's trying to do is make life a little easier for women. That doesn't mean she wants the world to be full of prick-less men."

"I guess that does sound ridiculous. But I got her and my ma saying different things, and now I'm all mixed up about who I should listen to."

"You should listen to Melinda." Here, at least, was safer ground. "You and your wife just do what seems best for your family, Johnny. And I can't imagine you tell your mother when you and Melinda are intimate, so it's not like anybody else has to know."

The relief was evident in the way Johnny's coloring eased back to normal and how he stopped shuffling his feet and stood up. "Thanks, Doc. I feel a lot better now, but I can't stay. Mrs. Carter's supposed to run over the Mercantile to get some things for Mrs. Digger, so I need to get back."

"Anytime you need to talk, you come find me," Will said, but he was already trying to think of something—*anything*—he needed from the store.

When Johnny was gone, Will grabbed his hat and headed toward the Mercantile. *Damnation*, but he felt like a boy sneaking out behind the schoolhouse to kiss a girl. It seemed like there just wasn't any other way to see Eliza Jane without telling the entire town the doctor and the women's libber were up to no good after they'd all gone to bed.

She wasn't in the Mercantile when he arrived, so Will looked over the new shipment of ready-made shirts. Then he looked at boots, then knives, then a whole lot of other things he had no use for. He was randomly flipping through the pages of the *Sears, Roebuck and Co.* catalogue when the bell over the door rang.

He didn't turn to look, instead turning another page and pretending to look interested. Through the corner of his eye, he watched Tom Dunbarton finish measuring out a pound of coffee and wander over to him.

"Feel pretty under your clothes, do you, Doc?" the storekeeper asked.

Will slammed the book closed when he realized he'd been pouring over a page of women's foundation garments. "I'm...researching the back-support features of corsets."

"I'll just bet," Tom replied, and then he looked over Will's shoulder. "Howdy, Mrs. Carter."

Will was about to turn around when she stepped up next to him at the counter, managing to brush her hip against his in the process. "Hello, Mr. Dunbarton. Mrs. Digger asked me to get the items on this list for her."

She handed over the note, and when he left to measure out the flour, Will reopened the catalogue to a random page not featuring unmentionables so he could bend his head in Eliza Jane's direction.

"I'll leave the back door unlocked tonight."

"I'll be there," she whispered.

A woman and her daughter stepped up the counter, ending the conversation. But it had served its purpose, so Will closed the catalogue and tipped his hat at the ladies before leaving empty-handed.

He was standing in the sunshine, pondering how to spend the hours until Eliza Jane came calling, when a wagon came careening into town, the driver shouting for the doctor.

ജോരുഷ

Will wasn't home when Eliza Jane snuck up his back stairs, so she whiled away some time exploring his private living quarters.

It didn't take long. There were two rooms, not counting the water closet—a main room with a kitchen area on one side and a sitting area on the other, and his bedroom. Austerely decorated, it didn't suit Will nearly as well as his office did. He was also either meticulously neat or did little but sleep there. She suspected the latter.

An hour passed before she started to worry. She'd peeked into his office earlier and his bag was gone, so she knew he was with a patient somewhere. But by the time the long hand of the clock ticked past the twelve for the third time, she was pacing the length of both rooms.

It was after midnight before the heavy tread of his boots on the stairs woke her from the light doze she'd fallen into. She sat up straight in the rocking chair and wiped the sleep from her eyes just as he stepped into the room.

"I didn't think you'd stay," he said, heading to the lamp on the table to turn it up a bit.

"I was worried about you," she replied, rising to give him a kiss hello.

Dark circles stood out against the pallor of his skin, overshadowing his blue eyes. He looked scruffy and exhausted, but he managed a small smile for her.

"The population of Gardiner has grown by one baby boy, and both he and his mama are doing fine."

He said it lightly, but she knew it hadn't been an easy birth. She could see it in his face, in the slope of his shoulders. Being the only doctor around had to be hard on him, and she felt a little guilty for being there in the middle of the night.

Now that the worry over his prolonged absence had been eased, Eliza Jane knew she should go, but she couldn't bring herself to leave him alone in his current state. He was too exhausted to take care of himself.

"Are you hungry? Did you eat anything at all while you were gone?"

He only shrugged and sank onto a chair to tug his boots off.

"I'll heat you up some beans," she said, moving toward the cookstove. "Not the best supper to have in the middle of the night, but they'll stick to your ribs."

She chattered inanely while she worked. She got nothing but the occasional grunt in response, but she didn't mind. Keeping him awake long enough to eat was the point, not being social. When she set the bowl in front of him, along with a slab of buttered bread, Will revived himself enough to dig in with relish.

He said nothing, focused as he was on lifting each bite to his mouth. When he was done, Will pushed back from the table and walked to his bed. He let himself fall face down, fully clothed but for his hat and boots.

"Thanks, darlin'," he muttered, and seconds later he was snoring.

Eliza Jane spent a few minutes quietly cleaning up after his meal, such as it was. While covering the butter crock, it struck her what a sweet picture of domesticity she currently made. The little woman taking care of her man with barely a proper thank you.

It was the basic principle she'd devoted her life to fighting, yet all she felt was a deep sense of satisfaction. Did that make her a hypocrite? Was it wrong to urge women to throw off the chains of domestic slavery when even now she was possessed of a deep sense of feminine pride she'd been there to see to Will's needs when he was too tired to see to them himself?

The questions made her feel jittery in the pit of her stomach, so Eliza Jane grabbed Will's broom and set about sweeping up the dirt he'd tracked in. With the lamp dimmed, she was probably doing a poor job of it, but at least her hands were as busy as her mind.

Maybe it was the man who made the difference. If he weren't so exhausted, Will would have shown a great deal of appreciation for the dinner. Or he'd have cooked it himself. Because Will Martinson was a man who knew all about appreciation—it was about all he received for taking care of Gardiner's ailments. Why, just last week he'd spent half a day tending to the injuries a man had sustained during an accident at the mill, and all he'd received was a jar of preserves.

When she'd expressed her shock at how little people rendered for his services, he'd said in that annoyingly laid back way of his, "Ah, but you've never had Mrs. Thurman's preserves, darlin'."

She'd pressed him, and he'd confessed there were a great many families in Gardiner who paid him with something other than cash. Sure, some had money, but others plied him with baked goods or mending or the thankfully rare offering of livestock. She was watching his face when he tried to explain that when a baby's fever broke and his or her mother looked in his eyes and said "thank you", that gift of gratitude was the purest and truest form of payment he could receive.

Eliza Jane tried to imagine herself in five years, waiting up and worrying about Will and then cleaning up after a midnight meal. She hadn't minded it tonight—in fact she'd been proud to care for him—but how would she feel if it became the extent of her life?

She leaned the broom against the wall with a sigh. It wasn't a problem to be pondered in the middle of the night, and she had to sleep if she was going to make it through the workday tomorrow. After pressing a light kiss to his forehead and turning down the lamp, she snuck back out and crept through town, the hotel hallway and into her room.

ಸಿಕಿಂಚ

Will woke the next morning to a vague memory of Eliza Jane tucking him into bed and a summons from Miss Adele delivered in the form of a note slid under his door.

He cleaned up, changed clothes and made a quick stop at the restaurant for a small breakfast and a lot of coffee. Adam had come and gone, so he ate alone, then headed for the Chicken Coop.

He kept an eye out for Eliza Jane as he made his way down the sidewalk, but she was nowhere to be seen and the livery corral was empty. When he was finished with Miss Adele, he'd have to track her down and apologize for the previous night.

Hellfire. He'd left one hell of a bad impression. She'd come for a little romancing, and instead she'd fed him and put him to bed. He couldn't remember if he'd even said thank you. It was certainly no way to endear himself to a woman who thought men didn't know how to appreciate a woman.

But then again, it wasn't altogether a bad thing to have happened. The fact remained there were times when this was how his life was, and maybe it was best she'd seen it now— before they started getting even more involved than they already were.

Miss Adele was waiting for him in her room, her hair done and her face made up, as always. But there wasn't enough paint in the entire Coop to hide the pain in her eyes and the lines around her mouth.

"Good morning, beautiful," He perched himself on the edge of her bed. "To what do I owe the pleasure of your invitation?"

"I've received a letter from my niece Rebecca." She handed the folded paper to him. "Read it to me, William. My eyes are tired and my little chickens can't read."

He unfolded it, cleared his throat and started to read. "My dearest Aunt Adele... It is with the most bittersweet of emotions I received your letter. As my father recently passed on, leaving me destitute and with no prospects, the timing seems a Godsend. While I am unclear as to the exact nature of your business, I assure you I am a quick study and adept with figures.

"It saddens me greatly to know that this opportunity comes to me at your expense, however. I remember with great fondness your visits when I was a young girl.

"I humbly accept your generous offer, Aunt Adele, and I shall make great haste in my preparations to leave in the hope we may be reunited before your health takes a turn for the worse. Your loving niece, Rebecca."

Will refolded the letter and gave Miss Adele a chiding look. "You didn't tell her you run a whorehouse, did you?"

"I admit to being a little vague on the details."

"Running a house full of women who have sex with men for money is not the kind of business you spring on a young lady who's done nothing but care for her father for the last fifteen or so years."

"You read it yourself, William. What other choices does she have? Giving herself to a husband she doesn't love just to keep a roof over her head? That's not the life I want for my niece."

"And being a whorehouse madam is?"

"It's done fine by me." She coughed—a horrible, wracking cough that left bloody flecks in her fancy handkerchief. Will's gut clenched. She was getting worse in a hurry and he feared she had little time left.

"Before my sister passed on," Miss Adele continued, "Rebecca was a little firecracker after my own heart. She was a feisty one, very forward-thinking and adventurous. But after... I've kept tabs on her, you know, through friends. Living with that gloomy, boring son of a bitch has buried her spark. And if she has to turn around and marry somebody else just like him in order to survive, that little spark will just die out completely.

"I'm not saying the Coop won't come as a shock. But maybe that spark will come to life and she'll be the woman she was *meant* to be. Maybe she'll walk away from the whole thing. Maybe she'll sell it and use the money to find a new life. But this way she'll have a *chance*, William. She'll have a choice."

He squeezed her hand, though not as tightly as the sadness was squeezing his heart. "Sounds like she used to be just like you, darlin'."

She laughed softly, then had to wait for another coughing fit to pass. "Oh, she was. If she gets her temper up, she'll turn this little town on its ear."

"Well, ain't that just dandy. Just what Gardiner needs—another strong-minded woman raising hell."

Of course she knew exactly who he was talking about. "Whew, that Eliza Jane sure is a pistol, ain't she? She'd make a mighty fine wife for you, William."

"Now you know pink isn't flattering to my handsome complexion," he teased, but in his mind he was picturing a tangle of naked limbs. Candlelight reflecting in pale blue eyes.

Tell me how it feels, darlin'.

It feels so...right.

Miss Adele tapped a fingernail against the back of his hand. "I do believe she would be the perfect friend for my Rebecca, too."

"Eliza Jane will be moving on soon, and it's best everybody remember that." Especially himself.

"Oh, that girl's not going anywhere."

"Have you taken up tea reading, woman?"

"I don't need to read dregs in the bottom of a cup when the writing's on the wall for anybody smart enough to open his eyes and see it." More coughing. "I sure would like to see you married before I die, William."

"I adore you with all my heart, Miss Adele, and you know it. But if you're even thinking about making my marrying Eliza Jane Carter your deathbed last wish, I'll smother you with a pillow. Now you think about what that will do to that fancy face paint of yours before you say another word."

She didn't have the strength to laugh again, but she squeezed his fingers. "Now, William, you know I want to look pretty when I die."

He had to strain to hear her now, and the ache burned like turned cider in his belly. "You need to rest, darlin'."

"That I do. I'm just going to drink this medicinal thing you made me and then close my eyes." She was whispering to avoid triggering another spell. "Be kind to Eliza Jane and make my Rebecca welcome. Watch over my sweet chickens."

With a certainty that made his throat close up, Will knew she'd made that drink a lot more medicinal than he'd given her instructions for. *I want to look pretty when I die.*

He made himself stand up and kiss her cheek like always. She was burning with fever. "I love you, Adele."

"I love you, too, William, as if you were my own son. Now you go on and let a lady get her beauty sleep."

Will left her door open. He didn't want her to be alone for too long.

Chapter Ten

A knock on her door woke Eliza Jane from a deep sleep. Utterly exhausted after the previous night and the day's work, she'd fallen into bed in just her robe and had been asleep before her head hit the pillow.

"Who is it?" she called, trying to shake off the grogginess. She was honestly too tired to even hope it was Will.

"It's Fiona, Miss Carter. From the Chicken Coop."

Eliza Jane retied her sash before opening the door. The pretty woman's eye makeup was smeared, and her eyes and nose were red from crying. "I'm sorry to disturb you this late, but Miss Adele has passed on earlier today."

Will. He'd be devastated. "I'm so sorry for your loss, Fiona. Is there anything I can do?"

"Well, us chickens, we got each other. But Doc Martinson, he's bad off about it. He's in his office and...there ain't nothing we can do for him. I thought maybe you'd go."

"Isn't Sheriff Caldwell with him? They're good friends and—"

"No disrespect, ma'am, but when a man's grieving that bad, he don't need a friend. He needs his woman."

"I'm not..." *...his woman.* "I'll get dressed and go right over. And thank you, Fiona, for coming. You'll let me know if there's anything I can do for you or the other ladies?"

"You're a good friend to us, Miss Carter. That's already more than most will do," Fiona said sadly, and she closed the door behind her when she left.

Eliza Jane slipped out of her robe and into a blouse and skirt, not bothering with anything else. It was late and nobody would see her out on the street. She just needed to get to Will.

Her heart broke when she stepped inside his office, dropping the bar across the door behind her.

In the glow of one dim lamp, she could see the half-empty bottle of whiskey. Tears flowed unchecked from his red and raw eyes, and hoarse sobs occasionally caught in his chest. The grief was almost palpable, as if the entire room had been draped in a blanket of sorrow.

She went to him without speaking and wrapped her arms around his shoulder, pulling his head to her stomach. He nuzzled his face against her, his fingertips digging into her hips. The muscles of his back quivered under her hands and she kneaded them, trying to ease the tension she felt in him.

"I'm sorry," she whispered.

She wore only the thin, white blouse, so she felt his face press against her skin, hot and damp. She realized his fingers were pulling at her skirt, bunching it up into his fists.

He needs his woman. Eliza Jane started at her collar, unfastening the row of tiny buttons she'd just barely finished fastening. When she reached his head, she paused to run her fingers through his hair. He pulled back enough to look up at her, his blue eyes full of sorrow.

He stood, knocking over his chair. Tucking his hands under her arms, he lifted her and she wrapped her legs around his hips. He carried her into the back, into the exam room, and lowered her to the narrow bed.

Since she'd forgone undergarments in her haste—and perhaps her knowledge of what comfort he'd seek—he settled between her thighs and fumbled with his fly. She raised her hips to accommodate him.

Will groaned as he entered her, pressing his face into her neck. She ran her hands over his back and into his hair, soothing him and urging him on. His pace quickened and Eliza Jane wrapped her arms around him.

With a broken sob, Will thrust harder, his body letting out the raw emotions he couldn't express. She held him as his body shuddered, twitched, and then fell still. A few moments later he rolled off her, pulling her into his embrace even in his sleep.

Eliza Jane stared up at the ceiling. She'd just let a man use her body for his own comfort, with no regard to pleasure. And coming after last night, it should have offended her to her very bones. Instead she was as content as if she'd been the one to find release.

She was beginning to fear it was more than friendship and his character that made her not resent his need for her. Maybe it was love that made a woman not mind when there was a little more giving on her part and a little more taking on his.

Will's hand twitched on her breast, his sleep light and restless. She stroked his hair and started to hum. She avoided hymns and popular standards he may associate with the war and hummed instead an old lullaby she vaguely remembered from childhood.

As she stroked his hair, he stilled and started to snore softly. She held him for another hour before she silently slipped away.

୫୦ଽଠ୯ଓ

Late the following morning, Eliza Jane took a bracing breath and knocked on the door of the grandest house in Gardiner. Beth Ann opened the door, as always looking as pretty as a peach. Her creamy complexion paled slightly, and Eliza Jane realized the girl might misconstrue this visit as being about that Joey fellow she believed herself in love with.

"Is Mrs. Barnes receiving guests?" Eliza Jane asked when the girl only gaped at her.

"I...I'm sorry. Yes, please come in."

She'd been counting on good manners getting her in the door, so she was a bit surprised when a shrill voice demanded, "What are you doing in my house?"

"Good morning, Mrs. Barnes."

"Beth Ann, you go on to your room. I don't want you anywhere near this woman."

The girl fled, but not without casting a curious glance over her shoulder. Of course, she wasn't really a girl. She was a nineteen-year-old woman being totally stifled by her mother. But that was an observation for another day—her business was far more pressing than that.

"You," that mother hissed when her daughter was gone. "How *dare* you come here? I don't want you in my home."

Another deep breath. "You and I are going to come to an understanding, Lucy Barnes. And then I'll not darken your doorstep again."

Lucy crossed her arms and said nothing, which Eliza Jane took as a reluctant invitation to speak her piece. "I'm sure you've heard Miss Adele passed on yesterday."

"The death of an unrepentant sinner brings me no sorrow, Mrs. Carter."

Well, Mrs. Carter was better than Jezebel as far as names went. A glass of lemonade was probably still out of the question, though. "I would imagine so. She meant a great deal to Doctor Martinson, however, and he means a great deal to this town."

"I won't permit a service for that woman in our church, if that's what you're getting at."

"Miss Adele often spoke of her wish to be buried in the church cemetery, under the trees." The chickens had told her as much when she'd stopped by to check on them that morning.

But Lucy was having none of it. "She belongs out behind the blacksmith's with the other sinners."

Eliza Jane blew out an exasperated breath. "As a favor to the doctor who serves this town selflessly, we'd like for the church to offer a plot. I'm not asking the congregation or the reverend to come and shed false tears over her grave—just to be allowed to bury her behind the church."

"Have you spoken to Reverend Phillips about the matter?" Lucy demanded, her eyes narrowed.

"You and I both know you'll be the one to make the decision, Mrs. Barnes."

The woman got a little gleam in her eye at Eliza Jane's acknowledgment of her power in Gardiner. "Give me one good reason why I should allow a fallen woman to rest eternally among our good Christian dead."

There were undoubtedly some good passages in Lucy Barnes's Bible about forgiveness and mercy, but Eliza Jane didn't care to swap scriptures with the woman.

"Because if you allow Miss Adele to be buried in the church cemetery, Sheriff Adam Caldwell will escort Beth Ann to the town social in two weeks."

"You're lying," Lucy breathed, but the shrewd look in her eye turned hopeful.

"Sheriff Caldwell is a particular friend of Doctor Martinson's, as you well know. I spoke to him not an hour ago, and he said he'd be pleased to escort Beth Ann to the social if you'd do his best friend this one good turn."

Pleased was a slight exaggeration. In fact, the sheriff had threatened to shoot her, Lucy Barnes, Will *and* himself before she wore him down enough to listen to reason. Woe to anybody who thought to make trouble in Gardiner today. His trigger finger had still been twitching when she left his office.

"Let me pour some lemonade," Lucy offered, gesturing toward the sofa. "Please, have a seat."

The negotiations took nearly an hour, fueled by the most incredibly over-sweetened lemonade Eliza Jane had ever had the misfortune to drink. The reverend would not conduct a service nor would the Bible Brigade attend—the hypocrisy of such a showing would have angered Will, anyway. The chickens would be allowed inside the white picket fence to say their final goodbyes. Future visits were a sticking point, but they'd finally agreed on the plot being closest to the fence so the chickens could reach through the pickets should they want to leave flowers in the future.

So Miss Adele would be buried in well-tended earth under some of the few pretty trees in town. And Beth Ann Barnes would be escorted by Sheriff Adam Caldwell to the town social.

Four days later, Will had to do some fancy bargaining, but he managed to finagle enough flowers from the chickens to make a presentable bouquet. And since Eliza Jane had been busy helping the chickens with the funeral, working, holding meetings and doing God only knew what else, he went straight to the livery stable to deliver them.

She was mucking out a stall when he arrived, and she grimaced when she saw him standing there watching. Not exactly the reception he'd been hoping for.

"I brought you flowers," he said, holding the handful of colorful blossoms out to her.

Eliza Jane laughed, tucking a stray strand of hair behind her ear. "Here I am ankle-deep in horse sh...manure, and you brought me flowers?"

"Eliza Jane Carter, you almost said horse shit!"

"I did not," she snapped primly, but her lips were twitching. He only folded his arms—careful not to crush the bouquet—and waited. "Fine, I almost did. I think that just proves what a bad influence this town is on me."

Will grinned and started toward her. "The town or the doctor?"

"Both. You're *all* incorrigible."

"Guilty. But we're growing on you, admit it. You like it here."

"Well, I *have* realized my girlhood dream of shoveling out horse stalls."

He reached out and drew her into his arms, not giving a fiddler's damn who was watching. "I came here to thank you, darlin'."

"For what?"

He kissed her soundly before answering. "For...hell, woman, I can't even list it all. For feeding me beans in the middle of the night when you'd been expecting lovemaking. For comforting me when Miss Adele died even though I acted like a fool and went for the bottle instead of you. For facing down Lucy Barnes on behalf of an old whore you barely knew just because I loved her. For standing by me and the chickens at her funeral. For...that might be it for right now, but I'm sure there will be more."

"That *is* quite a list." She tipped her head up to smile at him. "But I didn't mind a bit of it."

Will pulled her down beside him on a hay bale. "How is that, Eliza Jane? I've been doing a whole lot more taking than giving the past few days."

"I don't mind it because I know you'd do the same for me. And because nobody's ever brought me handpicked flowers before."

He held the bouquet out to her. "I reckon I should have brought some water for them."

"I have a tin cup over by the pump I can put them in. And I'll look at them while I work."

Work. He knew it was a bad idea, but he couldn't help himself. "When are you going to stop this, darlin'? This is no kind of work for a woman."

She gave him a glaring look. "Don't you start with me, Will Martinson. Neither Mr. Digger nor Johnny have any complaints with my work, I'll have you know. And it sets a fine example for other women to see me holding my own."

"I just don't like seeing you wear yourself out."

She laughed and slapped his knee. "If I were to quit, what would keep you and Sheriff Caldwell amused while you stand around eating penny candy?"

Will leaned over to nip at her earlobe. "That's the highlight of my day, darlin'."

"Keep that up and I won't bathe before I come in for my next examination, Doctor."

He wrinkled his nose. "Barn smell doesn't really put me in the mood, but it ain't enough to keep me from touching you."

They were silent for a moment, and Will knew it was time for him to go. Eliza Jane had work to do, and he was keeping her from it. "How about you and I have dinner at the restaurant this evening?"

She arched an eyebrow at him, then looked down at the flowers. "Aren't you worried about being seen *keeping time* with the women's libber?"

"Not more than I'm worrying about not getting enough time to keep with you."

"And I suppose I'm not really a women's libber anymore, am I?" She laughed, but to Will's ear it wasn't a particularly happy sound. "I'm a stable girl, which is entirely more respectable."

"You're still a damn women's libber," he growled. "And you're still no end of trouble. But there ain't no reason I can't sit at a restaurant and share a meal with you. Of course, we might want to be a little more discreet about what I plan to have for dessert."

"Hush! What if Johnny hears you?" The harshness of her tone was set off by the curve of her lips. "I'll have dinner with you, but you have to go now so I can earn my pay."

And as simple as that, the light moment dimmed for Will. The reminder she was earning money so she could hightail it out of Gardiner hit him in the gut and it took all he had not to let it show.

"I'll be there at six," he said, and then he kissed her goodbye.

The thought of Eliza Jane leaving town stayed with him through the rest of the day. He thought about it while he walked to the restaurant. He even thought about it while he sat at the table, waiting for her to arrive.

Will was starting to think about marriage, and she was still thinking about leaving. And he didn't have a damn clue what to do about it.

Eliza Jane was surprised by the number of people in Marguerite's when she arrived. She usually ate her dinner an hour earlier than Will had specified, and must be gone before the dinner rush, she supposed. The crowd of cowboys, businessmen and others was predominantly male, with a few families mixed in, but she spotted Will right away. He was talking to a rough-looking, barrel-chested man.

The man was standing, as if he'd been walking past when he saw Will, so she made her way toward the table. It didn't seem likely they'd be discussing personal medical issues in a busy restaurant. The man departed just before she reached them, however, so Will was free to stand and give her one of those smiles that made her toes curl.

"Good evening, Mrs. Carter. I'm glad you could join me."

The words, and the formal tone he used, caused Eliza Jane to once again become aware of her surroundings. People were a little more still and a lot more quiet than when she'd just entered. Obviously their fellow diners were a little curious as to why the damn women's libber was sitting down to a meal with their doctor.

"Thank you for making the time to see me," she said a little too loudly. "I hope a discussion of recent medical advancements in the field of feminine reproductive disorders won't affect your appetite."

While men around them cleared their throats, shifted in their chairs and returned to their suitably manly conversations, Eliza Jane took her own seat and glanced at the slate where the daily specials were written. They had beef stew listed and, after the day's work, her mouth watered just thinking about it. If not for Will's presence, she'd order a big bowl for herself.

Will sat as well, his grin letting her know he was rather amused by her audacity. She was about to say something when Marguerite bustled up to their table.

"Look, it is my favorite customer," she said in her effusive, slightly-accented way. "You are so good for my business, Mrs. Carter! The wives, they make such a fuss about cooking that the men, they pay me to do it instead."

Eliza Jane smiled as Will rolled his eyes. She ate all of her evening meals at the restaurant, and the owner always made a fuss over her. "You're certainly busy tonight, Marguerite."

"Yes, it is wonderful, no? Now what will I bring for your supper?"

Eliza Jane looked to Will, and after a moment he raised his gaze from the menu. "It's customary in these parts for ladies to go first, darlin'."

Flustered, Eliza Jane felt the heat rise in her face. "Oh, I...where I come from it's customary for a man to order for the women in his party."

"Is it customary for the man to read a lady's thoughts to know what it is she's of a mind to eat?"

"She's of a mind to eat what he orders for her." Aware of Marguerite waiting patiently, Eliza Jane handed back the menu she hadn't bothered to read. "I would love a bowl of that beef stew, please."

Will ordered a steak and potatoes, and after Marguerite left he propped his elbows on the table and shook his head. "I reckon I'd be a women's libber, too, if I had to stand for somebody telling me what I was of a mind to eat."

Eliza Jane laughed, then tried to change the subject. She didn't want to think about Augustus Carter or her father tonight. "Who was that man you were speaking to when I arrived? I don't think I've seen him before."

"That's Roland Thayer." Will paused to take a sip of his water, and she used that moment to conceal her reaction to the name. "He's on the road a lot, driving his freight wagon, and I asked him to look in on a family that lives about fifteen miles north of here. They're doing fine, which is good to hear."

She nodded, but couldn't think of a single thing to say. She knew Roland Thayer was out of town for several days each week because those were the days she visited with his wife, Dandy.

Eliza Jane had finally run into her at the Mercantile, and Dandy had invited her to stop by the house, but it could only be on the days her husband was away. The woman still refused to admit Roland had ever laid his hands on her in anger, but Eliza Jane knew fear when she saw it. And Dandy Thayer was very, very afraid of her husband.

"That's...kind of him."

Will nodded, seemingly unaware of the awkward silence. "He seems a decent sort. The Thayers live on the outskirts of town. The house ain't much and Dandy hardly ever ventures out, but he'll do me the occasional favor."

"So you don't know his wife well?" She realized belatedly the question might seem odd. "I mean, it seems everybody knows everybody else's business in Gardiner."

"That's true, for the most part. But the Thayers have always been quiet folk who prefer to be left alone, and we respect that."

Eliza Jane was watching him closely, and he didn't seem to be harboring any troubled thoughts regarding Roland Thayer. And she knew if Will had evidence Dandy was being mistreated, he wouldn't stand for it.

And yet, she couldn't quite bring herself to press him on the matter of the Thayers. She couldn't prove Dandy was being mistreated when she denied it herself, and it was too risky to involve the law with no evidence. While it was easy to forget at times, Will was Gardiner's deputy sheriff and the sheriff was his best friend.

No matter how fair they seemed in their dealings with the townspeople—Sheriff Caldwell's penchant for shooting people aside—it was too great a risk to confide in them yet. The last time she'd asked the law for help had cast a shadow she couldn't outrun.

"It's good the other family's faring well," she said awkwardly, trying to close the door on that particular conversation.

By the time their food came, the uncomfortable moment had passed and she ate with relish. Perhaps it wasn't ladylike to mop up the dish with a second slab of buttered bread, but the appetite she worked up at the livery each day wasn't exactly ladylike, either.

In between bites of his steak, Will amused her with stories from his own day, launching into one about the sheriff after they'd pushed their empty dishes off to the side.

It seemed Adam decided to pay a visit to Mrs. Digger, the wife of the man who owned the livery stable. He claimed he was just feeling sociable, but every person who walked by the house could smell the rich, sweet aroma of fresh cookies in the oven. Unfortunately, Lucy Barnes was also of a mind to visit Mrs. Digger, so the sheriff claimed an urgent need to visit the water closet.

"Now, Mrs. Digger knew he was hiding from Lucy," Will said, "so she didn't say a word. That poor son of a gun spent almost an hour hiding in Mrs. Digger's water closet."

Eliza Jane's stomach ached from laughing so hard after a full meal, and she had to use her napkin to dab at her eyes. "He must have been mad as a hornet when he got out of there."

"Oh, he was. He told me if he'd known Lucy was going to talk Mrs. Digger's ear clean off, he'd have taken the cookies in there with him."

"Why doesn't he just surrender and marry the girl? He might have Lucy Barnes as a mother-in-law, but at least he wouldn't be hiding in water closets in this kind of heat."

"He's a stubborn cuss and he don't aim to ever marry. Besides, not many know this, but Beth Ann's set her sights on a cowboy her ma don't approve of."

Eliza Jane thought back to her brief conversation with the girl. "Joey, right?"

Will looked surprised, and then his eyes narrowed. "Yeah, Joey Keezer. You aren't encouraging that girl to do something stupid, are you?"

The cheerful atmosphere of the dinner faded away and she sighed in disappointment. "Do you really think I would tell Beth Ann to run away from her family?"

"I'd like to believe you wouldn't, but it wouldn't be the first time you've taken me by surprise, darlin'."

"Don't you *darlin'* me, Will Martinson. When Beth Ann Barnes confided her troubles in me, I told her eloping wouldn't make her happy and she'd best talk to her mother about her feelings, and keep on talking about them until the woman saw reason." She heard the snappish tone of her own voice and she regretted the conversation had circled around to unpleasantness again.

"Don't be upset with me, Eliza Jane," Will said, but when he stretched out his foot to touch hers, she jerked hers back, tucking both feet safely under her chair.

He frowned and leaned forward. "When you go around encouraging women to know their minds and act on it, don't be surprised by somebody thinking you might have encouraged a young woman to know her own mind and act on it."

"There's a big difference between teaching a woman to care for her own health and finances, and encouraging a young woman to ruin her future." She couldn't decide if she was more angry or more sad he'd thought her capable of such a thing. "And furthermore, despite what everybody seems to think, I do not go around lecturing to cause discontent and get everybody *riled up*. I do it so that maybe in the future girls like Beth Ann won't ever have to feel the way I felt."

Much to her horror, she couldn't see Will anymore through the blur of tears. Oh, good Lord, she was crying in the restaurant. As if they hadn't been enough of a spectacle simply dining together.

She was aware of Marguerite approaching and Will pressing money for their meals into her hand.

"But Mrs. Carter? Is she not well?"

"She's well enough, except for having a jackass for a dinner companion."

"Whatever you did, you had better be sorry, young man, or I'll give you a whack with my mixing spoon."

"I intend to make it better, Marguerite. And I'll try to do it right since I stitched up the last cowboy you took after with it."

Eliza Jane dabbed at her face with her napkin before allowing Will to lead her out of the restaurant. The cooler night air refreshed her a little, so she tucked her arm under his and they walked slowly down the sidewalk, just as they had her first day in Gardiner.

"I got thrown away, too, you know," Will told her in a quiet voice. "My family tossed me aside because I stood up for a cause I believed in. I know it's not quite the same, and that making your way's easier on a man, but the people who were supposed to love me turned away because of something in me I couldn't change."

She sniffled and edged a little closer to him. "When I heard Augustus's new bride was expecting, I was devastated. It was the lowest moment of my life, and I'd never felt so worthless or so hopeless. An acquaintance invited me to a suffrage meeting she was hosting, and...oh, Will, the things that speaker had to say.

"The strength of her convictions shone through with every word she spoke, and the message was so powerful. Can you imagine women being allowed to vote—to have a say in not only our own lives, but in the governing of our country? I wanted to define my own destiny, and I wanted to be strong and unafraid, like she was. It was as though I had a gaping hole in my life and this...this *purpose* filled it."

"I understand that, darlin'." He stopped in front of the hotel and turned to face her. "But sometimes a hole that seems filled is really only patched over."

She really didn't want to think about that too much right now. "Are you coming up?"

"Not tonight. You're about done in, and we haven't exactly been discreet tonight."

"I don't know how your family could cast aside a man like you." Damning discretion, Eliza Jane reached up to caress his cheek. "They must be complete and utter fools."

"As is Augustus Carter, a fact for which this lucky man is extremely grateful."

He turned his face to kiss the palm of her hand, then he tipped his hat and walked away, whistling a jaunty tune that made her smile.

Chapter Eleven

Several days later, Eliza Jane left the livery after the morning feeding and walked up the sidewalk. She had no idea what she was supposed to do for the chickens, but since she'd promised Miss Adele she'd tend to them, she made her way to the Coop to see if they needed anything.

She'd been in town long enough to know ten-thirty in the morning was the ideal time to pay them a visit. They'd be up and about, tending to their chores. But not yet beginning the long process of dressing, curling, painting and powdering themselves for their customers.

She found the four of them in the kitchen, sitting glum-faced around a table that bore an account book, writing implements, and a carved wooden bowl full of money.

"Good morning, ladies," Eliza Jane said, and it seemed as though they all sighed at once.

"We can't make no sense of this, Mrs. Carter." Fiona waved a hand over the table.

Eliza Jane settled herself in the empty chair. "What are you trying to figure out?"

"Well, we've got all this money here and we don't know how to split it up." As was usually the case when they were in a group, Fiona did the talking. She pulled a sheet of paper from the book and slid it across the table to Eliza Jane. "Here's the list Miss Adele wrote of who gets what, but we can't figure the percents."

"I know she was concerned about how you'd fare. Didn't she explain all this to you?"

"Yes, ma'am. We tried to pay attention, but I guess we didn't listen enough."

"Figures make my head ache," Betty added, and Sadie nodded.

Eliza Jane looked over the paper. Apparently the women, instead of keeping what they earned, put all of their money in the dish, and then Miss Adele divvied it up. There was a percentage to the house, a percentage to Miss Adele personally and a percentage to each of the chickens.

"We been putting it off," Fiona said, "but the bowl is full, plus we need our pay. You're plenty smart, Mrs. Carter. Can you help us?"

"Yes, I can, until Miss Adele's niece arrives." She desperately hoped that situation would work out well in the end. Will had told her Rebecca Hamilton had no idea what she was in for. But she'd claimed in her letter to be good with numbers, at least.

After practically suffocating her with relieved gratitude, the chickens scattered and Eliza Jane got to work. While she wouldn't go so far as to say she enjoyed arithmetic, she did like exercising her mind.

And though she certainly wasn't an expert in the financial affairs of houses of ill-repute, the percentages the girls received seemed more than fair. Eliza Jane also found the accounts the Chicken Coop maintained with other businesses and dug in, losing herself in the numbers.

When she finally looked up from the ledger, rubbing the back of her stiffening neck, she saw Will. He was leaning against the kitchen doorjamb, watching her.

"How long have you been there?"

"Long enough to think it's time you head to my office for a *special* examination," he said with a suggestive raising of his eyebrows.

Eliza Jane laughed and pushed the ledger off to one side. "I had no idea you felt that way about arithmetic."

"I happen to find smart women sexy as hell, plus you chew on your bottom lip when you're thinking. As the town doctor, I feel it's my sworn duty to kiss that better for you."

"Doc, is that you?" they heard Sadie call. "You're late!"

It was Eliza Jane's turn to raise an eyebrow, but there was nothing suggestive about it. "It sounds as though you already have an examination scheduled, Doctor."

"Jealous, darlin'?" She was, but she wasn't about it admit it. "Holly has a sliver near her shoulder blade, and they're all too squeamish to pull it out for her."

"How on earth did she get a sliver *there*?"

Will grinned. "I can demonstrate for you later, if you like. I'll just need you naked and a wood-paneled wall."

Warmth seeped through Eliza Jane as she imagined just how a man, a naked woman and a wall could lead to a sliver in her back. "Oh my."

"I do like when you say that—gets me all riled up. I bet you've never made love in a whorehouse, have you?"

Her cheeks flamed just at the thought. "Not nearly as many times as you have, Will Martinson. Now I have bookkeeping to finish and you have a sliver to pull. If you should see Fiona, send her to me, please."

Will pushed himself off the doorjamb. "I will, but as soon as you're done here, you stop by my office for that examination."

"Is Mrs. Carter sick?" Fiona asked from behind him, and Eliza Jane wanted to hide her face in her hands. "I'm sorry I asked you to see to the books if you're feeling poorly."

"She's just fine," Will assured her. "She's just suffering from a persistent itch she can't seem to scratch."

Eliza Jane almost choked on her sharp intake of breath. The audacity of the man!

But her indignation didn't keep her from dwelling on that itch the entire time she was helping Fiona count the money into the appropriately sized piles. After promising to spare a few minutes for the financial chore each day until Rebecca arrived, Eliza Jane practically ran out of the Chicken Coop.

Will was sitting at his desk writing in his journal when she walked in, slightly out of breath from her quick step down the sidewalk. Since the office appeared to be empty otherwise, she locked the door behind her.

"I can't believe you told Fiona about...itching and scratching," she said, hands on her hips.

He closed his book and set it aside. "Darlin', there ain't a damn thing I can tell that woman about scratching an itch she don't already know."

"She doesn't know about *my* itching."

Will leaned back in his chair and grinned up at her. "No, but the chickens have scratched a few of mine in the past, and I reckon it hasn't escaped their notice I haven't been to the Coop since you stepped off that stage. Except for doctorin', of course."

Eliza Jane decided to ignore the *in the past* part and focus on the present. "Are you planning to examine me from that chair, Doctor?"

"As a matter of fact I am, darlin'. Why don't you step out of your drawers and come over here?"

A shiver tickled her spine. How could a man with such a slow, lazy grin be so intense at the same time? "Just my drawers?"

"Yes, ma'am. And since the curtains are drawn and the door's locked, don't be shy about it."

That didn't really matter as she was able to shimmy out of her undergarments without lifting her skirts too high. But she could tell by Will's expression they were about to do something she wouldn't want all of Gardiner watching.

"Tell me, Eliza Jane, have you ever ridden a horse astride?"

What an odd question, especially considering the circumstances. "Rarely, but yes, on occasion in a relatively private setting."

"Good. Come here, darlin'." He held out his hand, and she took it, quite unsure of what was expected of her.

When she was standing directly in front of his chair, Will released her hand and gathered up the front of her skirt so he could reach behind her knees and pull her forward until she straddled his lap.

She gasped when her more sensitive body parts rubbed up against his denim-clad erection. "Will, what are you doing?"

"Enjoying myself, darlin'. See, I've had this particular fantasy in which I'm sitting here doing some book work when that damn women's libber comes in and distracts me by proving a woman can be on top just as well as a man."

And then he reached down between their bodies to unbutton his pants. She gasped when he slid into her and she instinctively rocked, taking him deeper with each downward thrust.

Will kept one hand on her hip but used the other to grab the back of her neck and pull her head down so he could kiss her. Their breath mingled as she moved her body over his.

"That's right, darlin'. Just like riding a horse."

She smiled and rotated her hips in a small circle, making him moan. "Giddy up, Doc."

He lifted her hips and pushed them down again, over and over until she bit into his shirt to keep from screaming his name and he groaned as he spilled himself into her.

The chair creaked as they both went limp, and Eliza Jane hoped it held out long enough for her to get the strength back in her legs.

"Damnation, woman, you're going to be the death of me," he whispered against her cheek. "But in my professional opinion, we should definitely schedule you for a follow-up examination."

"Whatever you say, Doctor."

༻꧁꧂༺

A week later, the day of the town social dawned much the same as every other day in Gardiner, Texas. Scorching hot and dry as a drunk's mouth the morning after. But as Will made his way toward the restaurant for some breakfast, he could feel the air of anticipation running through the town.

Today was the day Sheriff Adam Caldwell was going to step out with Beth Ann Barnes, and Lucy Barnes had made sure the entire town knew it. No doubt the smitten Joey Keezer had heard it, too.

Tom Dunbarton from over at the Mercantile was running a wager pool on how long it would be before somebody got shot. Will had put a half-dollar on two and a half hours.

As he drew near the Chicken Coop, he noticed Sadie out tending the flower pots. She was dressed in a simple flowered dress and her face wasn't all done up. While it was understood they wouldn't participate in the dancing except with one another, even the chickens turned out for the social.

"Mornin', Sadie," Will said, tipping his hat when she looked up.

"Hello there, Doc." She finished pinching off a dead blossom and stood. "Fine day, isn't it?"

"It is. You're all faring well, I hope?"

"As well as can be expected, I reckon. We sure do miss Miss Adele something fierce, and it'll be nice when Miss Rebecca comes."

"She'll be along. I sent a few telegrams out to the stations so she won't arrive expecting her aunt to meet her." He felt the familiar pang of loss, but it was easing a little because he focused on how full a life the madam had led and how she'd faced death on her own terms. He sorely wished she could have held on to see her niece, but he also knew the pain had been about as bad as she could stand toward the end.

"Miss Carter's been real kind to keep the books in the meantime," Sadie said when the silence dragged on. "Ain't none of us got a head for numbers."

"That's real nice. And how have you been feeling?"

"Just fine, Doc. I can hardly even tell I got a baby in me." But she rubbed her hand protectively over her stomach just the same. "Dan offered to marry me."

That he hadn't known, so it must have been a recent development. "Dan O'Brien, from over to the hotel?"

"Yeah. He's always been a particularly regular customer of mine. He's sweet on me, you see. And he's got it in his head this child might be his."

But it also might not be. "Are you considering his offer?"

"A fine businessman like that don't need to go marryin' a whore." She tried for a devil-may-care expression, but Will saw the sadness in her eyes. "Besides, Mrs. Barnes would see to it he got run out of town if he did such a thing."

Seeing Sadie happily married and a good mother to her child would have made Miss Adele a happy woman. And he himself wished the best for her, too. "Lucy Barnes ain't the only opinion in town, Sadie. And I reckon Dan considered all that before he proposed. If he's willing to offer, there ain't no good reason why you shouldn't accept."

She only shrugged, so he pressed on. "If he's that much of a regular, you know the kind of man he is, and you already told me he's sweet on you. Look at you blush, sweetheart. Are you a little sweet on him, too?"

"I wouldn't mind marrying Dan," she admitted, rolling the dead flower between her palms. "But he wouldn't be able to hold his head up in town for long, and the time would come he'd hate me for it."

He had to agree that was a strong possibility. "Maybe you could leave Gardiner. Go someplace new where you'd just be Mr. and Mrs. Daniel O'Brien and you could raise your baby together."

Sadie shook her head, the picture of sorrow and regret. "He sets great store by that hotel, as he should. It's a fine place and I can't ask him to give that up. I ain't worth that."

He put his finger under her chin and tipped her face up. "Don't you ever say that to me again, Sadie. You're beautiful and kind and you've managed to take care of yourself in a world that dealt you some hard knocks. You deserve some happiness."

She shrugged, and then changed the subject. "You escortin' Mrs. Carter to the social, Doc?"

Unfortunately it was a sore subject. "No, I'm not. She said she'd go alone and she *might* save me a dance."

Sadie shook her head. "You know she's just trying to save trouble for you. There's still some people that don't like her, and they especially don't like her spending all that time here at the Coop lately. But there ain't no other men turning her head, if that's what you're worried about."

He wasn't worried, exactly. It was a just a matter of the natural progression of their relationship. He felt it was time they step out in public and make their courtship known. Of course, they were a little further in the progression seeing as how they'd skipped ahead to the lovemaking, but they didn't have to make *that* known.

"I need to go help Holly with her hair now," Sadie said. "But I'll see you later at the social."

The social would start in the afternoon, giving the men time to see to their chores and the women time to see to their hair and finish their pies. Will and Adam volunteered every year for the pie-judging contest. When there was a ribbon at stake, the ladies could turn out some mighty fine baked goods.

There would be games for the young'uns and horse racing. Ugly as he was, Adam's horse was always favored to win and he usually did if his rider wasn't off shooting somebody. Then there would be a potluck dinner and music and dancing. If enough cowboys came in from neighboring spreads, there'd be some bare-knuckle brawling, too.

Hell, maybe they wouldn't even need the cowboys for that. With Adam, Eliza Jane, mourning chickens, and a gloating Lucy Barnes with her Bible Brigade all in one place, the brawling might see to itself.

He tipped his hat to Sadie as she went inside, and then continued walking, his mind still on Eliza Jane. Whether she showed up on his arm or not, he planned to make his intentions toward her very plain today. The people of Gardiner needed to start coming to terms with the fact their doctor was getting sweet on the damn women's libber.

Chapter Twelve

It was a good plan, but harder to set in motion than he'd anticipated. Will didn't see Eliza Jane at all for hours, and then, when he did, it was always from a distance. It seemed she was always talking to somebody or helping somebody set up tables. Carrying food.

And just when it appeared he'd get a chance to talk to her, somebody would waylay him, wanting to talk about the weather, the horse racing or their various aches and pains.

It wasn't until they were setting up for the pie judging contest he finally managed to pull her aside. "Are you avoiding me, darlin'?"

"Of course not. I'm very busy, and I really need to get my apple pie out to the table."

He tried not to look or sound as shocked as he felt. "You entered a pie?"

"You don't have to sound so surprised," she snapped. "I thought it might help me become more welcome in certain circles if I engage in a more womanly activity and Marguerite let me borrow her oven."

"No offense, darlin', but you don't strike me as the baking kind."

"I'm not, but I felt compelled to make the effort." She smiled ever-so-sweetly at him. "And you're one of the judges."

"Eliza Jane Carter, are you implying I'll cheat just because my boots have spent the night under your bed?"

"Never. But while you're taking a bite of my pie, you probably won't be able to help recalling there are womanly activities I *am* good at."

Will laughed, and wished he could kiss her right then and there. "You are a schemer, Eliza Jane Carter. But you're probably right, since I can't help recalling that fact every minute of the day as it is."

But fifteen minutes later, lovemaking was the furthest thing from his mind. He'd survived treating deadly and contagious diseases, the war between the states and being branded a traitor by his friends and family, but he didn't think he had it in him to survive his first bite of Eliza Jane's apple pie.

He forced himself to keep chewing. Her crust was about as tender and flaky as a dried-up chicken bone and gritted between his teeth. Something crunched against his back molars even as his cheeks started sucking in at the tartness. The woman might be generous in her lovemaking, but she was stingy as hell with the sugar.

He noticed Adam getting to his feet next to him, and for a second wondered if the fearless sheriff was actually fleeing from Eliza Jane's pie.

But he wasn't. Despite agonized taste buds and watery eyes, Will noticed the commotion over by the display of quilts. He took a gulp of milk before he stood, hoping it would soften the mass in his mouth enough so he could swallow before he had to speak. Eliza Jane wouldn't take kindly to his spitting her pie into the dirt.

A brawl was definitely brewing. Will listened to a half-dozen shouting people trying to explain the situation all at once. It seemed one of the chickens had hung a knitted blanket—at least it *seemed* to be a blanket—along with the other quilts.

Apparently the blanket was Sadie's and the quilt was Beth Ann's and the blanket was deemed unfit to be keeping company with the quilt. Whether that was due to Sadie's being a whore or the fact Adam's horse could likely knit a prettier stitch, Will couldn't tell.

But the ladies of the Chicken Coop and the ladies of the First (and only) Gardiner Church had started exchanging words. Dan O'Brien had rushed to Sadie's defense, causing Lucy Barnes to practically pick up her scrawny, henpecked husband and toss him into the mix.

Now the tall and gangly Dan O'Brien and the short, yet still fairly gangly, Brent Barnes were faced off, looking like a battle of bobbing Adam's apples.

"Shut up!" Adam roared, and the whole town fell silent. Even the hogs penned up for the greased pig event later stopped their squealing.

"You all squawk more than a pen full of chickens," he said, but then he turned to the four whores gathered together. "No offense, ladies."

Fiona gave him a saucy wink, but Sadie looked close to tears. Will was unfortunately still chewing, and so was unable to offer any words of comfort.

"You people interrupted the pie judging," Adam informed them, and since he didn't sound too happy about it, Will assumed he hadn't actually taken a bite of Eliza Jane's pie yet. "Now, what we have here is a town social. Not the town brawl or the town brouhaha. So you all go on and be social now, dammit."

"Sadie's got a right to display her wares," Dan O'Brien said, and Will admired the man's gumption. He must have been more than a *little* sweet on Sadie to talk back to the sheriff like that.

"Her *wares* ain't fit for decent society," Brent Barnes responded with a sneer.

Will could see Adam's right hand starting to twitch, so he swallowed the sour lump of pie, hoping he didn't choke. He'd barely gotten it down when Dan worked up the nerve to take a swing.

"I aim to marry her!" The man plowed his fist into Brent's face. Unfortunately he had the body weight of a sun-starved sapling and the other man only took one staggering step before striking back.

The next thing Will knew, O'Brien and Barnes were rolling around in the street like two twigs caught up in a dust devil.

Women and children squealed while the men roared their approval.

The crowd gave a single, horrified gasp when Adam drew his pistol. Will was about to step in when Lucy Barnes hauled off and slapped the sheriff with the good Book so hard his hat flew off and landed in the dirt.

"Don't you shoot my husband," she boomed like a clap of righteous thunder.

The entire town—even the brawling men—froze like stunned statuary as Adam whirled, bareheaded, to face Lucy. She lifted her Bible—whether she meant to ward the sheriff off or hit him again, Will couldn't tell.

"Mama!" Beth Ann cried in a high-pitched squeal. She pressed the back of her hand to her forehead and fainted.

Fiona, acting purely on instinct Will guessed, stepped forward and caught the girl as she fell. She held her for a moment, then she must have realized who she was holding because she made a face like she'd bitten into Eliza Jane's pie and Beth Ann landed in the dirt with a thud.

"I knitted that blanket for my baby," Sadie said, her plaintive voice damn near breaking Will's heart. Excitement rippled through the crowd—few had known one of the chickens was expecting.

"It's a beautiful blanket, Sadie," Eliza Jane assured her, and she gave Lucy Barnes a stare that practically dared the woman to say something mean.

But Lucy was too busy wondering if she was about to get shot to pay much mind to Eliza Jane. Adam had picked his hat up out of the dirt and was slapping it slowly against his thigh. He glared at the woman and she swallowed hard each time a puff of dust escaped it.

"Don't you even think about shooting me, Adam Caldwell," she warned, though her voice wasn't quite as forceful as usual.

"Oh, I'm thinking about it, all right, Mrs. Barnes."

Will figured it was about time for him to step in. There were too many conversations going on at once, and not one of them friendly. "Okay, everybody. We're supposed to be having a celebration here. Let's get back to it."

"You aim to marry a whore?" Brent Barnes demanded of Dan O'Brien, as if Will hadn't even spoken.

"I do," the hotel keeper declared for the whole town to hear. "If I can convince her to have me."

That statement was enough to distract even Adam. All heads swiveled in Dan's direction, and Lucy—no doubt eager to escape the sheriff's cold stare—lit right into him.

"You can't marry a...a...fallen woman!"

"Will all due respect, Mrs. Barnes, I reckon who I marry ain't your concern."

Lucy clutched her Bible to her chest. "You, sir, are a business proprietor in this town and the financial welfare of Gardiner is everybody's business."

Dan looked anxious as all get out and he kept casting nervous glances at Brent Barnes, but he didn't back down. "It ain't like travelers will think it odd the hotel owner has a wife. And I don't reckon any of them will be any the wiser about Sadie's previous occupations iffen you don't tell them. And being concerned about the town's welfare as you are, you wouldn't do that, now would you, Missus Barnes?"

Oh, he had her there, and Will thoroughly enjoyed the way she worked her mouth soundlessly like a gaping fish before stalking back to the pie table.

Damnation, he'd forgotten about the pies. Unless a tiny twister had come and sucked up Eliza Jane's pie during the brawl, going back to that table was just about the last thing he wanted to do.

"Ain't no reason I can't marry Sadie, iffen she'll have me," Dan reiterated, seemingly to the town at large.

"But...but..." Tom Dunbarton seemed to have something he wanted to say, and Will had a good idea of what it was. Being down to three chickens could be an inconvenience to the men in Gardiner. Since pointing that out could lead to another ruckus, thus keeping them all away from the pies a little longer, Will hoped he'd say it.

Instead, Dunbarton came to his senses. "But...somebody oughta pick Beth Ann up off the street now."

"I'm going to eat pie," Adam declared, thunking his well-beaten hat back onto his head.

"Sheriff Caldwell," Eliza Jane said, and Will groaned. She had no concept of minding her own affairs, and she was using that *I aim to be stubborn as a mule* voice. "Seeing as how you're Beth Ann's escort for the day, shouldn't you offer her assistance if she's feeling poorly?"

Even Will would have squirmed under the look Adam gave her. "Since I caused her to faint, Mrs. Carter, I'm hardly the right person to revive her."

And he walked away. Beth Ann was already starting to stir on her own, and her father went to help her up, giving Dan O'Brien a thunderous look as he went past.

The crowd began to disperse, and Will had no choice but to return to the pie judging table.

He held his breath as Adam bit down into his first bite of Eliza Jane's pie. The sheriff's eyes widened and Will winced at the fact even *he* could hear the crunching of the crust between the man's teeth.

Adam chewed slowly and cautiously. Will watched, hoping he wouldn't have to choose between his best friend and the woman he...was sleeping with. The sheriff's temper was already high, and breaking a tooth on a pastry wouldn't sweeten it any. Especially considering Eliza Jane's light hand with the sugar.

She was watching the sheriff with a hopeful expression, but Will knew—judging by his own experience trying to swallow his mouthful—that she'd be waiting a while. So he improvised and frowned at a distant spot over Eliza Jane's shoulder.

She turned and Adam spat the wad of crunchy, sour pie into the dirt between his boots, then scuffed his foot over it. When Eliza Jane turned back to give Will a questioning look, he smiled.

"I thought I saw something going on over there. Guess I was mistaken."

Adam made a big show out of swallowing nothing, drawing her attention back to him. She clasped her hands, that hopeful smile lighting up her face again.

"That sure is some pie, Mrs. Carter," the sheriff said after taking a healthy swig of milk.

"Did you like it?"

"Ma'am, a pie like that makes a man wish he had a pick axe and spade so he could *really* dig into it."

Will figured the happy look on Eliza Jane's face made having to swallow a bite of her pie worthwhile.

In the end, Tom Dunbarton's mother took first—as she had since the very first Gardiner social years ago—and they gave Eliza Jane third behind Lucy Barnes because Will did, in fact, like how his boots looked under her bed. Adam wanted to give her the second place ribbon on account of Lucy knocking his hat into the dirt, but they were afraid the woman would demand to taste the pie that beat hers.

As it was, during the flurry of activity following the contest, Eliza Jane's pie managed to disappear. When she took notice, he and Adam made a big show of rubbing their bellies and grinning, but she didn't look quite convinced.

Will hoped it was almost time for the dancing to start so he could distract her. He was going to bring up a subject that would chase all thoughts of ribbons and apple pies right out of her head.

ೞ෩ಅಞ

Eliza Jane threw back her head and laughed as Fiona tried to lead her for a third time through the steps of a high-spirited dance.

It was scandalous, of course, to be dancing with one of the chickens, but she didn't care. To ban the women from kicking up their heels in public with the same men who paid them for sex struck her as ridiculous, so she flouted their stuffy conventions.

And, if she were to be honest, she'd have to admit she was enjoying watching Will watch her. He'd been nearby all through the festivities, keeping a possessive, watchful eye on her. It thrilled her to know that, while most probably thought he was simply following the sheriff's order to keep her out of trouble, she knew he was counting the hours until she was naked and under him again.

Fiona whirled her around and Eliza Jane laughed again. The town social had been one of the most enjoyable events she'd ever attended. She'd cheered on the men and boys trying to grab hold of mud-slickened pigs, and been amazed at how fast the sheriff's horse could run. He didn't look like much, but he had the soul of a Thoroughbred. And the food...she hadn't eaten so much in a long time.

Just as Eliza Jane was starting to get the hang of the dance steps, the so-called band changed to a much slower tempo that slightly—*very* slightly—resembled a waltz.

Will swooped right in, taking her hand from Fiona's. "I do believe you owe me a dance, darlin'."

She tried to hold him at a respectable distance, but Will was having none of that. He swept her into his arms and into a pattern that at least resembled a waltz far more than the music did.

She gave him a coy smile dredged up from her debutante days. "You're very light on your feet considering how much of my pie you ate."

He missed a step and they wobbled for a moment, then he fell back into the rhythm. "That *was* quite a pie, darlin'."

Will's hand kept drifting further down her back, and she squirmed, trying to draw his attention to it. With the entire Bible Brigade in attendance, he couldn't afford to give any appearance of impropriety. As far as she knew, Lucy Barnes hadn't rescinded her threat to have him castrating calves if he was caught misbehaving with the women's libber.

"You're drawing attention to us," she hissed when his hand came to settle on the small of her back.

"So let's find a little more privacy."

Privacy in the middle of the social seemed out of the question, so she laughed at him. "We'll have privacy later. For now, behave yourself."

But Will led her a little to the right with each turn, until they were on the far fringes of the dancing area. With the band playing loudly, if not well, they were out of earshot of the other dancers.

"Are you trying to get me alone, Doctor Martinson?"

"You know, darlin', if you'd marry me, we wouldn't have to sneak around trying to keep a secret half the town probably already knows."

Eliza Jane scrambled out of his arms so fast she almost fell on the ground. "If I *marry* you? What are you talking about?"

Will put his hands on his hips and smiled at her. "It's a ceremony. Preacher, ring, vows."

"Oh, I know all about vows," she snapped, looking around to see if anybody gave the appearance of eavesdropping. "That's the part where I promise to obey you until one of us is dead."

"You are one romantic woman."

"There's nothing romantic about the chains of matrimony." Good Lord, why did Will have to go and ruin everything by talking about marriage? There was nothing wrong with what they had—companionship, intimacy and independence.

No, it wasn't perfect. She didn't like the sneaking around any more than he did, but she couldn't stand the idea of giving up her identity once again. If she became Mrs. William Martinson, eventually she would become nothing more than the dutiful doctor's wife he wouldn't admit he was really looking for.

Not that any of it mattered. She was leaving soon, and that would be that. And speaking of leaving, the thrill of the social was now irredeemably diminished, and she considered returning to her room. But first she needed some water.

"Eliza Jane, look at me."

She didn't want to. One look into those blue eyes and she could be lost. Since she'd only recently begun to rediscover herself, she didn't care to lose herself again so soon.

But when he repeated the words again more softly, she turned and looked at him.

"Would it be so bad being my wife?"

She thought of all the times he'd been exasperated with her. There had been several times she knew he wanted to lock her in her room just to buy himself a few moments of peace. How long would he tolerate her independent and forward-thinking ways if he actually had the authority to enforce his wishes?

"I don't know," she said honestly. "And I'm too afraid to find out."

His eyes looked as sad as she'd ever seen them. "There's going to come a time when this won't be enough for me anymore."

She was saved from giving an answer she didn't have by the clamor being raised by the gathered citizens. Will walked past her without another word, leaving her to follow after.

Lucy Barnes was the center of attention—as usual—waving a piece of paper around while her husband sat on a bench fanning himself. What was unusual were the tears running down her cheeks.

"She's gone!" the woman was shouting at the sheriff, and Eliza Jane was shocked to see she didn't have her Bible in hand. Something terrible indeed must have happened.

"Calm down," Adam told her. "What do you mean she's gone?"

"She was upset earlier about fainting, so she went home to lie down. When I went to check on her a few minutes ago, I found this note. She's run off to marry some cowboy named Joey Keezer!"

Eliza Jane's gasp of surprise was lost amidst all the others. Beth Ann was gone?

"You'd better go after them right now, Sheriff," Lucy ordered, waving the paper under his nose. "You go get my daughter and bring her back."

Her earlier disagreement with Will slid to the back of her mind as Eliza Jane pondered Adam Caldwell's situation. Having Beth Ann married to somebody else would make his life immeasurably easier. But as the sheriff, did he have a duty to go after the runaways? She wasn't a child, after all, but a woman old enough to marry.

"Well, I reckon *Guapo's* pretty tuckered after winning the race earlier," Adam said slowly. "It might be best to head out at first light."

"*Guapo*?" Eliza Jane repeated, unable to help herself. "You named your horse *handsome*?"

His black eyes swung to focus on her. "I did. You see some reason why he shouldn't be called that?"

"I...um...he just didn't look Spanish to me."

"*You!*" Lucy Barnes shouted at Eliza Jane now that she'd gone and drawn attention to herself. "You're behind this, aren't you?"

Every head turned in her direction, and Eliza Jane was struck speechless by the accusation. While she supported independence and free thinking in women, she would *never* counsel a young girl to run off and elope with a cowboy.

Especially the daughter of Lucy Barnes. Good Lord, that was just asking for a heaping plate of misery.

"I had nothing to do with this," she finally managed to say, wondering if her hesitation made her look guilty in the eyes of others. Perhaps a little more... "I was under the impression Beth Ann and the sheriff here were practically betrothed and I certainly wouldn't stand in the way of his blessed matrimony."

Adam and Will both snorted, so she assumed that was a little *too* much. "Beth Ann didn't confide her plan to me, Mrs. Barnes. That's all I can say."

With the wind taken out of her sails on that regard, Lucy turned her attention back to the sheriff. "You go and fetch her back here right now."

He took the paper from her and gave it a quick read. "Beth Ann ain't a little girl, you know. She's old enough to go off and get married."

She stepped right up to him, though, being short, that meant she had to crane her head way back. "I don't think she run off with him. I think he took her and you'd best go get her back."

"Oh, for the love of God, shut *up*, woman!" Brent Barnes yelled, and the whole town fell silent.

She turned on him like a snarling wolverine. "How *dare* you speak to me like that, with our own daughter taken away from us and in danger?"

"She wasn't taken, and you know it. That boy and her have been courtin' since she was sixteen and you're just too stubborn to admit it. The only reason our daughter is gone right now is because it's the only way she could get a lick of happiness."

Eliza Jane wanted to cheer, but everybody was still silent, no doubt waiting to see what the sheriff would do if Lucy Barnes started beating her husband to death in the middle of the town social.

"I did *not* raise that girl to marry a good-for-nothing cowboy!"

"I was a good-for-nothing file clerk when we got married, Lucy. Do you even remember back then—back when we were young and in love and you didn't feel a need to *be* somebody?"

"This isn't about *my* happiness, Brent Barnes," she shouted back.

"Well, it certainly isn't about Beth Ann's." He turned to Adam. "You go on and enjoy the festivities, Sheriff. I reckon I'm still the man of this family and my daughter has my blessing."

He turned and walked away, but the crowd could hear Lucy henpecking at him all the way up the street.

As people went back to what they'd been doing, Eliza Jane turned to find Will looking at her. "I had *nothing* to do with any of this!"

"I know you didn't. Now come and dance with me and I'll try to behave myself."

Chapter Thirteen

Two days later, Eliza Jane was pondering whether or not to squander some of her hard-earned wages on a sour pickle when a short, leather-skinned woman with a straggly knot of hair and work-hardened hands marched over to her. It was hard to tell, but Eliza Jane thought the woman might have a wad of tobacco tucked into her cheek.

"You that women's libber what told my daughters how not to have so many young'uns?"

Eliza Jane sighed. She was exhausted and not in the mood to be accosted while pondering the wooden pickle barrel. "I am."

The other woman smiled, confirming her chewing tobacco suspicions. "Good. I had ten young'uns, one right after the other. Two died in birthin' and I lost three to sickness along the way."

"I'm so sorry," Eliza Jane's own woes faded into insignificance in the face of another's hardship.

"I played the hand God dealt me," the woman said without a trace of self-pity. "If my girls get to play a better hand on account of having an ace or two up their sleeves, then I'm all for that."

178

She wasn't sure she'd ever heard her cause described as cheating the Lord at poker before, but Eliza Jane understood the sentiment. "Making women's lives a little easier is all I try to do."

"Well, you're not a bad woman, no matter what them other folks say." And she walked out, leaving Eliza Jane to stare after her.

She couldn't possibly buy a pickle now.

The money she earned was supposed to be getting her back to Philadelphia, but she'd grown complacent. Instead of writing letters and reaching out to acquaintances in order to procure the means necessary to further her campaign, she was still in Gardiner, Texas, bookkeeping for prostitutes and carrying on a clandestine affair with the town doctor.

Making the lives of a few women easier wasn't enough. There were countless women in towns just like Gardiner waiting for somebody to show them how to make their world a slightly better place. And she was failing them.

Suddenly, she couldn't take a full breath and she pressed a hand to her chest. Doubt clouded her mind to the point she didn't think she could think straight.

Doing what she thought was right meant leaving Gardiner...and Will. And then there was Sadie and her baby. Would she marry Dan O'Brien? Would Beth Ann and Joey ever come home? Would the sheriff and his ugly horse ever find a woman to love them? There were so many people in Gardiner she'd hate to leave behind.

But especially Will. It was hard for her to imagine her life without him—his strength, his laugh. His touch. The pain of leaving him behind threatened to be even worse than the pain she'd suffered when her husband cast her aside—she'd never loved Augustus.

Maybe it was time to preserve the money she had and earn some more so she could head out of town before she and Will became even more attached to each other. That way, he could find one of those perfect doctor's wives he was talking about and she could continue her work.

He thought he wanted to marry her, but she could see it would never work out. She simply wasn't what he needed.

Why did doing the right thing always have to be so painful?

"Mrs. Carter, you all right?" Tom Dunbarton asked from behind the counter.

Belatedly realizing she was making a spectacle of herself in the Mercantile, Eliza Jane managed a wobbly smile. "I need a job."

"Thought you were working over to the livery? Not that I think you should be, of course."

"I am. I need a second job—more money. Do you need any help here in the store?"

He looked at her like she was plumb crazy, which she more than likely was. "I been thinkin' on hiring a young man to—"

"I can do anything a young man can do."

"Is that right?"

❸❹❸❹

With the day's general ailments behind him, Will had just propped his feet up and cracked open a recent medical journal when his door flew open damn near hard enough to rip it off the hinges.

"Do you see this?" Adam Caldwell demanded, holding up a bullet. "This one's got Eliza Jane Carter's name all over it, whether you're bouncing the bedsprings with her or not."

If the sheriff was looking for him to be shocked, he'd be sorely disappointed. The woman had been damn near begging to be shot since she'd arrived, and the sheriff damn near begging to do the shooting. He did look particularly vexed this evening, though. And Will had thought Adam was growing accustomed to Eliza Jane.

"What's she gone and done now?"

"It seems the idiot men folk of this town decided she could have a job at the Mercantile if she proved she could take her drink like a man."

Will let his feet slide to the floor with a thump. "I don't want to hear this, do I?"

"You'd better hear it, or you'll be hearing the gunshot. She's in the saloon right now, drinkin' down the liquor like she's at a goddamn tea party."

"Shit."

"I'm giving you a ten minute head start on account of us being friends."

Will didn't even grab his hat on the way out the door. The damn fool woman was going to be the death of him.

He heard the laughter and shouts of encouragement well before he stepped into the dimly lit saloon. Eliza Jane stood at the bar, surrounded by a crowd of men. Judging by her bright eyes and flushed cheeks, they'd been at this for a while before the sheriff caught wind of the goings on.

"Doc!" she yelled, raising her shot glass in a none-too-steady salute.

"Doc!" the crowd chorused.

"What in blazes are you doing?" he demanded.

It was Tom Dunbarton—a little pink-cheeked himself—who answered. "I'm gonna give Eliza Jane here a job if she can drink me under the table like a man."

"Well, if that ain't the most damn fool notion I've ever heard, I'll eat my hat."

"You aren't wearing it," Eliza Jane pointed out helpfully, waving her glass in what she probably thought was his general direction.

"Time for you to leave, sweetheart," Will said in his best deputy voice. No doubt Adam would be along very shortly.

"Ooh, are you going to give me another one of your *special* examinations?"

Every head in the saloon swiveled in his direction, but she was too busy giggling to notice.

"Eliza Jane," he warned.

"Doc likes to sit in his fancy leather chair and have me ride him like a horse," she cheerfully informed at least half the male population of Gardiner. "Giddy up, Doc!"

"Giddy up, Doc!" the crowd shouted.

Eliza Jane giggled, belched and then passed out cold on the floor.

Aw, hell.

಄ಬಬಬ

Eliza Jane didn't remember getting kicked in the head by a mule recently, but she couldn't think of any other way to explain the excruciating pain.

She knew with a certainty if she opened her eyes or tried to move she was going to lose whatever remained in her sour stomach.

"You awake, darlin'?"

"No," she whispered with cotton-dry lips, wishing Will didn't have to shout quite so loud. Cracking one eye just enough to get a glimpse, she realized she was in the narrow bed he kept for patients.

"Let me guess—pounding head, upset stomach, dry mouth? Think you're dying?"

"Yes." Maybe he'd cure her of it.

"Good. Maybe you'll think twice before you do something so fool headed again."

Up until that moment Eliza Jane had thought doctors were supposed to be compassionate, but this one's bedside manner was sorely lacking.

The front door to the office opened and then closed with a bang that nearly rattled the window loose. Eliza Jane moaned aloud and prayed for death.

"Good morning, Doc! Patient awake yet?" Sheriff Caldwell yelled, and there was a cheerful note to his voice that told her he knew exactly how she was suffering.

"She just woke up, as a matter of fact. Was thinking I'd send over to the restaurant for some runny scrambled eggs and maybe some warm milk."

Her stomach rolled and she gagged, but she kept down whatever evil concoction was burning up her stomach.

"I hate you, Will Martinson," she forced out in a croaky voice.

"Now that's funny," the sheriff said—*shouted*, "because just last night you were telling every man in the saloon how you ride the doc here like a horse."

Oh…good Lord. Moving very slowly and gingerly, Eliza Jane grasped the thin blanket Will must have given her and pulled it up over her head. With any luck people would mistake her for dead.

Glimpses of hazy memories returned. *Giddy up, Doc.* She'd actually said that right before things got *really* blurry—then dark. Poor Will.

She'd have to sneak out of Gardiner in the middle of the night. She could hide under the blanket until dark, steal a horse and ride like the wind. Assuming she could move by nightfall.

"What I want to know, Mrs. Carter," the sheriff continued, "is if you wore spurs."

His laughter sliced through her head and Eliza Jane whimpered.

"Goddammit, Adam," she heard Will say. "Are you here for any reason besides tormenting me?"

"You? Hell, I thought I was tormenting that women's libber of yours. I gotta say, she *is* one liberated woman."

"I may not be able to take you in a bare-knuckle brawl, but you're going to be damn sorry you said that next time you need doctoring."

"Now don't go getting up on your high horse, Doc."

"Adam, you—"

"Just sit tall in the saddle and it'll pass."

"Stop."

"You need to be a man about this or folks will start wondering if you've been gelded."

There was a scuffle that echoed through Eliza Jane's skull as if her head was a burlap bag and her brains were pots and pans.

"Dammit, cut it out, Will! Jesus, you've sure got a burr under your saddle blanket this morning."

There was more scuffling and male laughter, and Eliza Jane thought about lowering the blanket to see what was going on, but that would require movement. It would also let the light back in.

Finally, they settled down and turned to the real business at hand. Eliza Jane tried to hear what they were saying over the awful pounding in her head.

"Lucy Barnes heard all about last night and she's on the warpath," she heard Adam tell Will. "Word is she's declared you unfit to treat anything but diseased swine, and anybody offering your woman a job will be boycotted by the Bible Brigade. And she's convinced Dan O'Brien the wrath of God will descend and turn his hotel into a pile of scorched lumber if Eliza Jane spends another night under his roof."

She heard Will mutter a string of words she couldn't repeat, even in her own mind. But they did seem to sum up what she was feeling.

"Maybe she could stay at the Coop," Will suggested, which was even worse than the cussing in her estimation.

Eliza Jane genuinely liked Sadie and the other chickens, but taking up residence in a whorehouse was close to the bottom of the list of things she'd hoped to accomplish in her life.

"Dan and I had a little talk this morning," Adam said, and Eliza Jane pondered how busy everybody had been while she lay dying in the doctor's office. "And it seems Dan's more afraid of me than he is of God."

"Well, there ain't no stories in the Bible about God shooting a man just for calling his horse ugly."

"He lived. And my horse ain't ugly." There was a short pause. "Of course, as horseflesh goes, he ain't nearly as pretty as you."

When the sheriff's laughter finally died down, Will called out, "You still suffering, darlin'?"

She unglued her tongue from the roof of her mouth well enough to say she was.

"Good."

There was a little more conversation she couldn't quite make out, and then the sheriff left as boisterously as he'd arrived. She hated Adam Caldwell with a passion, whether he'd scared Dan O'Brien into keeping her or not.

"Why did you do such a thing?" Will asked, clearly talking to her now. There was no trace of the jovial ease with which he'd spoken to the sheriff.

She pulled the blanket down and opened her eyes as far as a squint. "I need another job. I need to make more money."

"So you can leave me."

His voice was so flat it almost hurt more than her head. "Will, I...you knew I wasn't staying forever."

"You know, Adam told me a while back you'd either stay here for me or you wouldn't. I guess he was right. A life with me is either enough for you or it's not, Eliza Jane."

Tears leaked from her puffy eyes, spilling over her cheeks, and she didn't have the strength to wipe them away. "It's not about you. It's not even about *me*. I need to make a difference."

"You make a difference *here*," he snapped, and his tone echoed through her head like a thunderstorm. "You make a difference to the chickens and to Melinda Barnes and a whole lot of other people. And me. I don't want you to go."

Why did he have to do this *now*—now when her head was screaming and her whole body hurt and she couldn't even think straight? "It's not enough."

He was quiet for a moment, and when he spoke again his voice was so sad she could feel her heart break. "I have to ride out to one of the ranches and check on some cowboys laid up with a fever. You think on it, and when I get back I'll give you the money to get whereever it is you think you'll be happy."

And then he was gone. Eliza Jane pulled the blanket back up over her head and cried. It hurt to cry and the sobbing wracked her sore body, but it couldn't even come close to the pain she was feeling on the inside.

Chapter Fourteen

Will had only been back in his office ten minutes when he heard the running boots on the sidewalk that generally signaled he wasn't about to enjoy peace and quiet anytime soon.

Ten minutes had been long enough to find the bed empty and realize he felt about the same. Empty and hurting and about as angry as he'd ever felt. Now he even gave a thought to going out the back door, getting on his horse and leaving it all behind—Gardiner, Eliza Jane and the ache in his chest there was no medicine for.

Before he could move, the door flew open and Tom Dunbarton was there, red-faced from exertion and excitement. "Doc, you best come. They need you out to the Thayer place. Seems Dandy started throwing around ideas she got from that women's libber of yours. Roland got into the liquor and he took his fists to her."

"How bad is she hurt?"

"I can't rightly say. But they're poor folk. Wouldn't call for a doctor unless they needed one. And Dandy took after him with her rolling pin. Chased him right out into the street. He might be dead, Doc. And you better hurry, because the sheriff and that women's libber are like to shoot each other iffen you don't."

Will's blood turned icy and he almost dropped his bag. "What the hell do you mean by that?"

"Miss Carter, she's got herself a shotgun. Says she ain't gonna let the sheriff near Dandy. And the sheriff, he's got his guns and he says there ain't no way he's going to let a crazy woman be what kills him. Damn, giddy up, Doc. We're missing it!"

Will ran all the way down the main street and off to the right where the Thayers' sorry excuse for a house stood. Where the hell had Eliza Jane gotten a shotgun? And he and Adam might have a good friendship, but the sheriff wasn't going to let himself get shot just because his friend was partial to the woman holding the gun.

Tom hadn't been exaggerating. Roland Thayer was sprawled in the dirt with a bloody head. Dandy Thayer stood on her front porch, holding a blood-smeared rolling pin. Eliza Jane stood in front of her, wielding the shotgun while Adam stood over Roland, guns drawn. Will should have known better than to leave her alone.

"Doc may never forgive me if I have to shoot you, Eliza Jane Carter," Adam was shouting. "But I ain't lettin' you kill anybody today, even if it means shooting a woman."

"You just stay back. This shotgun doesn't care that I'm a woman, Sheriff. It'll blow you out of your boots just as surely as if a man pulled the trigger."

Will walked slowly toward the men, until Dandy spotted him. "Don't you go near him, Doc Martinson! You let him lie there and suffer."

He saw Eliza Jane jerk when she heard his name, but she didn't lower the barrel of the gun. When she looked at him, he saw such a look of misery he almost felt bad for her. But there was a stubborn set to her mouth that told him she might not be the one needing the pity. He shook his head, still not quite believing the nightmare he could see with own damn eyes.

"Hush, Dandy," Adam ordered.

"Don't you tell me to hush, Adam Caldwell," Dandy shouted. "Don't you dare. I am *tired* of being hushed. I am tired of being told the stew wasn't salty enough and the shirts are scratchy and that I don't have the brains God gave a sheep. And I ain't gonna be hit no more, neither."

"Nobody's gonna hit you," Will said quietly. "But you've got to let me see to Roland or you might end up with more trouble than bland stew."

"My stew ain't bland."

"Sweetheart, listen." Will was taking slow, easy steps forward as he spoke. He didn't want to spook anybody, especially Eliza Jane. She still looked like hell and was a little unsteady on her feet. "You let me see to your husband. Let me get him fixed up first, and then—if he's been taking his fists to you—we'll lock him up."

But Dandy Thayer would have none of it. "You ain't gonna do nothing. You just want Miss Carter to put down that shotgun."

"I'll admit to not liking that gun being waved around, but I'm not lying about locking Roland up. Ain't that right, Adam?"

"I won't stand for a man hitting a woman," the sheriff said in a tone that told them he meant it.

"You won't shoot him, will you? Dandy asked, and Will wondered if maybe she was starting to feel some remorse. They'd been married a long time—their children were already grown and gone.

It took Adam a few seconds to decide. "Not unless I have to."

"Good, because if he's got to be killed, I aim to be the one who does it."

Will was watching Eliza Jane. Her arms were trembling, whether from the weight of the gun or fear, he couldn't tell. "You don't need that gun anymore, darlin'. Put it down on the floor next to you."

He was surprised when she actually did what she was told. "I'm sorry, Will. I was visiting and he came home. He was...so angry I was here and went to hit her and she grabbed the rolling pin. I...I just didn't want anybody to hurt her, and the gun was leaned next to the door."

Will didn't look at Adam as the sheriff moved toward the porch. Eliza Jane had found herself in a whole new kind of trouble, and Will had a patient bleeding in the dirt to tend to. Plus, she'd made it pretty plain she didn't need him after all.

"Mrs. Carter," he heard Adam say in a cold voice, "I need to talk to Dandy some more and help the doc see to Roland. I want you to go right now and sit in my office until I get there. Do *not* make me come look for you."

"I'll be there," she told him in about the smallest voice he'd ever heard from her, and it took a considerable amount of willpower to keep from looking up—from taking her in his arms whether she wanted it or not—as she walked slowly past.

৪৩৪৩৫৩

It was nearly three-quarters of an hour before Will and Adam stepped into the sheriff's office, and in that time Eliza Jane had recovered her composure and was ready for them.

She sat ramrod straight in a chair, her hands folded in her lap. She wouldn't cry—she'd cried herself out that morning—and she wouldn't cower. She didn't look at either man as Will took a seat near her and the sheriff sat behind his desk.

"Roland Thayer will recover," Adam said abruptly, "though he'll have the worst headache of his life. I won't be pressing charges against his wife."

She wanted to sag in her chair with relief for Dandy, but she didn't. "And will you keep your promise to lock him up for abusing her?"

"I ain't never made a promise I ain't kept, Eliza Jane Carter."

"Have you ever stuck around long enough to see the results of your work?" Will burst out, as if he couldn't hold the words in another second. "Or do you just ride in, get everybody riled up and then just ride right out again?"

"What happened today was not my fault, Will. I'm not the one who hurt Dandy. I didn't spend twenty years degrading her and beating her."

"She never beat him senseless with a rolling pin before you came."

Eliza Jane straightened in her chair, disappointment causing a keen pain in her chest. "So you think it would have been better if I hadn't come?"

"Darlin', you are no end of trouble."

"So it would have been better for Dandy Thayer to keep suffering in silence. Far better for her to be belittled and beaten for the rest of her life rather than cause a fuss. She should have remembered her *place* instead of lifting a hand to her husband in defense of herself."

"Goddamit, Eliza Jane! That is *not* what I mean."

"Yes, it is." She rose to her feet, looking down at the two men. "You're both angry with me because I told her she deserved better in life. Because I told her it was wrong that her husband treated her worse than he'd treat a mongrel dog. Because I told her she had a *right* not to be punched in the face because her husband's coffee was a little too bitter."

She turned, intending to make an emphatic exit, but Adam's tone of voice stopped her. "Sit down."

"I will not."

"Sit down or I will sit you down myself."

Eliza Jane laughed bitterly, but she sat. "I believe you would, seeing as how you both condone violence against women."

Adam crossed his arms and pinned her with his dark stare. "Did you tell Dandy Thayer she had the right to defend herself against her husband?"

She crossed her own arms and glared right back at him. "Yes, I did."

"Did you ever tell her that that the next time he tried to lay a hand on her, she should come to me?"

"In these cases, officers of the law often—"

"Did you?"

"No."

Will shifted in his chair. "Did you tell her she should bring her injuries to me so I could treat her and swear out a complaint against him myself?"

She looked down at her hands, surprised to find them trembling. "No, I didn't. She wouldn't admit it to me, so she wouldn't have admitted it to you."

"Did you think to come to me or Adam yourself and tell us you thought Roland Thayer was beating his wife and she needed help?"

"I went to the law once, on behalf of a woman who needed help." Eliza Jane felt the anger stirring in her all over again. "The sheriff bought her husband a few drinks and told him maybe he shouldn't beat his wife. And her husband, who got drunk, was convinced she'd shamed him by speaking out.

"He beat her to death that night. And maybe if she'd taken a rolling pin to his head instead of my going to the law, she'd still be alive."

"I ain't that sheriff," Adam snapped.

"How do I know that?" Eliza Jane snapped right back. "Better a woman learn to take care of herself than to place her trust in yet another man who may not do right by her."

"That's an awful lonely way to live," Will said, and the sadness in his voice was reflected in his eyes.

She didn't know what else to say. While there were maybe other choices Dandy could have made, Eliza Jane could only make decisions based on her own experiences. And her experiences with going to the law had been tragic.

The sheriff cleared his throat. "Right or wrong, there are going to be some people in this town who blame you for what happened to Roland Thayer. The man's got a lot of friends, and you're going to want to be careful. Keep your door locked and try not to find yourself in isolated places. Will and I can't be watching you every minute."

"I understand," she whispered, eyes on her lap. "I'll be careful."

"Look at me," the sheriff demanded, and she did, blinking away the tears. "I know you believe in what you do, Eliza Jane. And I know you intend to keep on doing it. You just need to remember that a woman not only needs to know she can change her lot in life, but she needs to know *how*."

She nodded, feeling very humbled. "I apologize for what I said about you condoning violence against women."

"Apology accepted." Adam got to his feet and put his hat back on. "And if you tell anybody I was soft on you after you pointed a gun at me, I *will* shoot you."

And then he left her alone with Will, and one look at his face told her the humbling had barely begun.

"You sure do make it hard for a man to love you, Eliza Jane."

"It's easier for everybody that way."

"I said you made it *hard*, not that it already hadn't happened. I love you and I want you to be my wife, despite your being a pain in the ass the likes of which I've never seen before."

She'd thought herself totally cried out, but her eyes welled up anyway. "We've talked about this."

"No, I've talked. You've tried to avoid it altogether." Will leaned forward in his chair, propping his elbows on his knees. "Do you love me?"

"Yes." The word escaped her lips before she could stop it. "But—"

"So give me a good reason why us lovin' one another ain't enough to keep you here."

Unable to look him straight in the eye, she looked at his hands and went for the easy answer. "You love children, Will, and I can't bear any for you."

"That's bullshit, Eliza Jane. In case you haven't noticed, I have an entire town full of children. Sure, I see the worst of them as a rule, but each of them is special to me. If I feel a need to throw a ball around with the boys or read a storybook to a little girl, all I have to do is step outside and give a holler."

"It's not the same."

"I won't feel the loss of not being a father anywhere near as bad as I'd feel the loss of not being your husband."

The word *husband* made Eliza Jane's heart ache for what could have been. "You said yourself I'm the opposite of everything a doctor's wife needs to be."

"But you're not the opposite of what *this* doctor needs his wife to be."

"You won't be happy with me for long, Will. And I won't change."

"You're not being fair to me. I've never tried to change you."

"You said I was no end of trouble."

"And that's the truth. But I fell in love with you anyway. So it seems to me if I want a stubborn, wanton troublemaker as a wife, you shouldn't be trying to talk me out of it."

She didn't know what else to say. She didn't know how to explain that she loved him so much she didn't see how she'd get through the rest of her life without him. And how afraid she was he'd wake up one day and realize she wasn't really the wife he'd wanted after all. She'd survived Augustus casting her aside, but couldn't survive Will not wanting her anymore. It would kill her.

While she sat silently, trying desperately to come up with the right words to convey her fears, Will stood and dropped a leather wallet onto the desk in front of her.

"I can't believe I'm helping you leave me, but that's enough to get you anywhere you want to go."

Eliza Jane lowered her face to her hands as she began to cry in earnest.

"I won't beg you to stay, darlin', but I also can't take any more of this. It hurts too much. You either get on the next stage out of town or you stay and be my wife. The choice is yours."

Will walked to the door, but paused and looked back at her. "I love you, Eliza Jane. Not the woman you think I want you to be, or the woman other folks say you should be. I love *you.*"

He closed the door behind him.

Chapter Fifteen

On the morning Eliza Jane would leave Gardiner, she woke to rain beating on the roof of the hotel. It seemed appropriate somehow that the sky would cry the tears she couldn't.

When she turned her head on the pillow, the first thing she saw was the single yellow blossom in the glass of water on the bedside table. Johnny Barnes had given it to her, to thank her for her talks with Melinda. Dandy had baked her a batch of muffins for her journey. She closed her eyes again, not wanting to see the evidence of how much the town—or some of it, anyway—had embraced her. And how much she'd come to care for them.

Her trunk was packed, so after dressing and stowing a few last things, she went down to the front desk and asked Dan O'Brien to have her things brought down front in time for the stage.

"I will, Mrs. Carter. But I wish you weren't leaving us." He swallowed, his Adam's apple bobbing. "And Sadie's going to miss you something fierce."

"I'm going to miss her, too. As a matter of fact, I'm going to walk down and say goodbye after I have breakfast."

She went to the restaurant, where she ordered coffee she barely sipped from and a meal she only picked at. When Marguerite handed her a picnic basket filled with food for her trip, Eliza Jane thanked her effusively and fled before she could break down and make a scene.

It was tempting to pay a visit to Lucy Barnes just to make the leaving seem easier.

Rain kept people indoors, so Gardiner seemed unnaturally quiet as she walked down the plank sidewalk, staying close to the buildings in an effort to stay dry. When she reached the Chicken Coop, she took a deep breath before opening the door. This goodbye wouldn't be easy.

At first she thought she'd missed the chickens entirely—perhaps it was shopping day—but she found Sadie in the kitchen, wiping dishes and putting them away.

"Good morning, Mrs. Carter," she said sadly. "You're still leaving today?"

"It's for the best, Sadie." She pulled out a chair and sat down at the table. "Where are the others?"

"Holly and Betty are upstairs in their room. They don't do well with goodbyes and they ain't comin' out. Fiona went to the Mercantile and to visit Miss Adele's resting place. She likes to walk in the rain and she doesn't want you to see her cry, I guess."

"I'm going to miss you all, Sadie. Who will do your bookkeeping? And I'm going to miss knowing how your life turns out and if you marry Dan and whether the baby's a boy or a girl and..." Her voice choked off and she shook her head.

Sadie put down her towel and took a seat across from her. "Dan's going to take care of our money for now. And I already plan to ask Miss Adele's niece to write you once she comes—if you let us know where you are. And as for Dan's proposal, I told him I won't make any decisions until after Miss Rebecca comes. With only the four of us, it don't seem right for me to up and leave, too."

"You know as well as I do the others would be nothing but happy for you if you marry Dan and get to raise that baby in a nice home."

"I don't know how to be a wife, Mrs. Carter. My momma died birthin' me, and my daddy wasn't no good, so I ran off when I was old enough, and I ain't done nothin' but whorin' since. I don't know how to be Mrs. Daniel O'Brien."

Eliza Jane reached across the table and covered Sadie's hands with her own. "He didn't fall in love with Mrs. Daniel O'Brien. He fell in love with you, Sadie. You're not a stranger he just met. He knows who you are and he knows what you've done."

"The only wifely thing I know how to do is give him pleasure in bed."

"Is it pleasurable for you, as well?"

"With Dan, you mean?" When Eliza Jane nodded, Sadie smiled. "He's a sweet man and he always tries to make our time together special."

"That's wonderful! And look how well you and the others keep up this big house. You can cook and clean and anything else you need to do. Being a prostitute is just one of the things you do. It's not who you are."

"Well, I hear tell you're leaving because you won't marry Doc on account of you being a women's libber. How is that different from me not marrying Dan on account of being a whore?"

Eliza Jane drew her hands back, shocked. "That's... It's an entirely different situation."

How on earth had Sadie heard about Will's ultimatum? She supposed he might have told Adam, but Sadie wasn't likely to have heard it from him considering the way he avoided the Coop as a rule.

Then she realized what a ridiculous train of thought that was. In Gardiner, everybody knew everybody's business.

"It ain't no different," Sadie insisted.

"It is," Eliza Jane said, perhaps a little more abruptly than she'd intended. "Prostitution was your job. The liberation of woman is my life philosophy. It colors everything I think and do and say. It's a part of who I am."

"Fancy words just confuse me, Mrs. Carter. You think women should be treated decent. I sleep with men for money. I think it's pretty plain which of us makes for a better wife."

"*Slept*, Sadie. You *slept* with men for money *in the past*." She didn't want to talk about Will and marriage. "You can start a whole new life—be a wife and mother, and help Dan run the hotel."

"Fiona told me I do have a strong background in hospitality," Sadie said, and they both laughed, though not for long.

"It don't matter now, anyway," Sadie continued. "I told him we'd wait 'til Miss Rebecca comes and then we'll see. If after waiting and listening to the townsfolk jaw about it, he still wants to marry me, I probably will."

"I hope you do. When a man is willing to defy the entire town by marrying a prostitute carrying a child who might not be his, that speaks to a pretty powerful love. Don't dismiss that too readily."

"I reckon a man wanting to marry a woman who can't cook, gets drunk in saloons and makes an entire town full of men so mad they could spit speaks to a mighty powerful love, too."

Heat prickled around Eliza Jane's collar. "We're not talking about me."

"Well, we wasn't, but now we are." Sadie leaned back in her chair and folded her hands over her softly-rounded belly.

"I'd never make a good doctor's wife."

"I reckon everybody knows that, especially the doc. But it's just like you told me about Dan falling in love with a whore and not a perfect wife. Doc Martinson fell in love with a women's libber, and not a perfect wife."

Eliza Jane was horrified to find her vision blurring from tears. "I'm afraid, Sadie."

"I've known Doc for years, Mrs. Carter, and he wouldn't ever hurt a woman."

"Not afraid of *him*. I'm afraid of...having it all turn bad. I know he loves me, and I love him. And we had our own independence while still having each other and it was working. What if becoming man and wife ruins that? I was a wife once, and it made me desperately unhappy."

"The way I see it is that the man made you unhappy, not the marriage. You ain't never been Doc's wife, but being his woman sure has made you happy, hasn't it?"

Eliza Jane smiled and wiped the tears from her cheeks. "You're a wise woman, Sadie."

"No, I just ain't real smart, so I don't overthink things the way you do."

How could a woman *not* overthink something like marriage? Willingly handing over the kind of authority to a man was something women didn't think about *enough*, in her opinion.

"Will loves you," Sadie said softly. "He could have his pick of any woman in Gardiner—or in any other town—and he chose you."

"I'm leaving today, and some day when Will has a nice wife and a pack of children, he'll thank me for it."

Sadie stood and shook her head. "Hell, maybe I *am* smarter than you. But I don't want us arguin' on your last day. Us chickens made you a goodbye present. Wait here."

She went down the hall and came back a moment later carrying the ugliest—and yet most beautiful—scarf Eliza Jane had ever seen.

"We all knitted on it," Sadie shyly handed it to her.

She could see they'd all taken turns. Fiona's tight, determined stitches. Sadie's rows, which varied in length as she randomly dropped or added stitches. Betty knit so loosely her rows had an almost lace-like quality, and Holly seemed to purl accidentally quite often. And it was bright red.

Eliza Jane pressed it to her face, inhaling the lingering perfumed scents of these fallen women as if she could keep them with her forever.

"We figured you might end up someplace cold, and we wanted to keep you warm."

Eliza Jane's raw eyes burned and she threw her arms around Sadie. "It's the most precious gift I've ever received. I'm going to miss you ladies *so* much. I...I have to go."

After one final squeeze, she looped the scarf around her neck, grabbed the picnic basket and left the whorehouse for the last time.

The rain had dwindled down, and Dan had set her trunk and valise out in front of the post office to await the stagecoach. It was almost time, so Eliza Jane sat on the trunk to wait. She'd said the goodbyes she could say.

She hadn't seen Will since he'd delivered his ultimatum in the sheriff's office, and she had nearly convinced herself it was for the best. But she couldn't stop thinking about him as the time drew near to leave.

He'd been right about not trying to change her. He hadn't interfered with her meetings, or with her working at the livery stable. He hadn't paved her way in Gardiner, but let her find her own way. He not only loved her, but he had respected her, as well.

And as she remembered how Sadie had thrown her own words back at her, Eliza Jane wondered if she was making the biggest mistake of her life.

A memory rose unbidden in her mind of the first time Will made love to her. *Tell me what it feels like, darlin'.*

It feels so...right.

Everything about Will Martinson felt right. It was she herself who was wrong.

ဆဝၭဝၗ

Will could see the post office from his window, and even though he'd told himself he wouldn't, he found himself drawn to it as the time for the stage drew near.

She looked so sad—so alone—sitting on her trunk, and he wanted to go to her like he'd never wanted anything else in his life. But it wouldn't do any good. She had made her choice, and he wouldn't plead with her in the middle of the street no matter how much he wanted to.

He'd stayed away from her since their last discussion in Adam's office. Not only because he wanted her decision to be made of her own free will, but because he was weak.

He may have thrown down the gauntlet, so to speak, but he was afraid if she pushed the subject, he'd let things go on just to keep from losing her. When he was close to her, he had more than a little trouble thinking straight.

But when he was away from her, that was when the frustration set in. He was tired of scheming up reasons to be alone with her. Giving her a smile and a nod when he passed her on the street wasn't enough for him. He wanted all of her, for better or worse. And so he'd stayed away from her.

The rain picked up just as he heard the pounding of hooves and rattling of harness that signaled the stagecoach, and he pressed his hand to the glass as she stood and picked up her valise.

Don't go, darlin'.

The stage rolled to a stop, blocking his view, but still Will stood and watched. He could see it rock as the passengers disembarked for a short break. The minutes ticked by endlessly, and then the stagecoach shifted again as the passengers climbed back aboard.

Only this time the woman he loved would be among them, and when the driver cracked his whip and the horses started to move, he wanted to run out into the street and hold onto it, dragging his heels in the dirt to slow it down.

But he just watched, silent and heartbroken as the stage gathered momentum and moved on down the street. He tried to look into the window—just one last glimpse of her—but the curtain was down. When the stagecoach was totally out of sight, he closed his eyes and rested his forehead against the glass until he thought maybe he'd kept the tears at bay.

When he opened them again and looked back at the post office, he saw her. She was still sitting on the trunk, a red scarf around her neck. Tears streamed down her face with the rain, and she was watching him.

He'd known this woman too long to feel safe being hopeful, but he couldn't help it. He damn near ripped the door off its hinges getting out of his office, and she was on her feet, too.

Mud in the street sucked at his boots as he crossed the street, and she met him halfway. She was rain-soaked, crying and smelled like wet wool and cheap perfume, but when she threw herself into his arms, he didn't care.

He held her hard and long, and he wasn't ever going to let her go. He had to clear his throat before he could speak. "Hellfire, woman. Are you *trying* to make me crazy?"

She pulled back enough to look into his eyes. "I love you, Will."

He used his thumbs to brush her wet hair from her face and tipped her chin up. "I told you if you stay, you have to marry me."

"And I stayed."

"Are you sure, because I can't go through this again."

"I am. Are you sure you won't wake up some morning and not want me anymore?"

"Oh, darlin', is that what's been going on in that head of yours?" He cupped her face in his hands. "How can *you* be sure you won't wake up some morning and not want *me*?"

"I'll never stop wanting you, Will."

"I'll *always* want you, too, Eliza Jane. I'm never going to let you go."

He kissed her thoroughly, standing there in the rain in the middle of the muddy street, and he didn't stop until he heard Adam clearing his throat.

"You people are disturbing the peace." Sure enough, a crowd was gathering. "And I ain't taking the Bible whacking for this, Doc. You wanna kiss your woman in the mud, you can dodge the brimstone your own self."

"We're getting married!" Eliza Jane shouted to the entire town and a cheer rose up around them.

Before his woman could be set upon by a flock of shrieking chickens, Will leaned close to whisper in her ear, "Maybe they'll even write songs about the day the women's libber vowed to love, honor and *obey* her man in front of God and Gardiner, Texas."

Epilogue

"Push, Eliza Jane!"

She groaned and pushed, putting her whole body into it before she had to stop and pant some more. "This is all your fault, Will Martinson, so why don't *you* push for a while?"

"Now, darlin', you know I have to stay at this end and pull."

Eliza Jane had no intention of forgiving Will for this anytime soon, and she'd been telling him just that for the past two hours. Sweat had plastered loose strands of hair to her face, and the ache in her body was growing too persistent to ignore. She was hot and tired, and didn't want to do this anymore.

"I quit," she declared with a note of finality.

"Darlin', you can't quit. Just a few more pushes and it'll come out."

"You put it in there. *You* pull it out."

Will stood up straight and put his hands on his hips. "It was your idea to come with me, so it's your fault I took the buggy."

Eliza Jane waved her hand at the mud caused by a sudden and fierce thunderstorm. The mud had the buggy stuck fast right up to the axles. "It wasn't my idea to drive though that."

"If you had stayed home, I'd have been riding. I was just checking on the boy's fever."

"We agreed going with you was a good way to meet more people and get them to like me, and the women almost always have questions for me they were too shy to ask you."

"Just push a little more."

"No."

Will took off his hat and slapped it against his thigh. "Woman, you are no end of trouble. Hellfire, just two weeks ago you promised God you'd obey me."

Eliza Jane smiled, even though the mud was now seeping over the tops of her boots. "No, I promised God I'd love and honor you. I had my fingers crossed for the obey part."

"Well, that explains the lightening." Will put his hat back on and returned to considering the buggy. "We'll never get it out in time to meet the stagecoach, and according to the telegram from Rebecca, she's going to be on it today."

"Maybe I should have stayed in town," she admitted reluctantly. "Adam's going to do a poor job of telling that girl her aunt left her a whorehouse."

"We'll have to ride the horse back to town and come back for the buggy with some mules later. It won't be comfortable without the saddle, but I don't aim to sleep in that buggy tonight."

A few minutes later they were heading for town, Eliza Jane seated in front of Will. He was right about it not being overly comfortable, so she leaned back against him, trying to shift herself a bit.

"You keep squirming like that, darlin', and you're going to get me all riled up. Again." Eliza Jane laughed and deliberately squirmed a little to the left. "Keep it up and, without the padding of a saddle, I'll wind up crippled forever."

"That's a shame. If we could go a little faster, we might have time to share a bath before the stagecoach arrives."

He nuzzled the back of her neck. "With that fruity bath oil that makes your skin all slick and soft?"

Good Lord, she loved being this man's wife. "I do have some of that left."

Will groaned and she felt his thigh flex as he gave the horse a little kick. "I reckon we could ride a *little* faster."

Eliza Jane laughed again as her husband wrapped one arm around her waist to keep her still. "Giddy up, Doc."

About the Author

Shannon Stacey married her Prince Charming in 1993 and is the proud mother of a future Nobel Prize for Science-winning bookworm and an adrenaline junkie with a flair for drama. She lives in New England, where her two favorite activities are trying to stay warm and writing stories of happily ever after.

You can contact Shannon or sign up for her newsletter through her website: www.shannonstacey.com

Look for these titles

Now Available

Forever Again
72 Hours
On the Edge
Talons: Kiss Me Deadly

Coming Soon:

Becoming Miss Becky

GREAT
cheap
FUN

Discover eBooks!
THE FASTEST WAY TO GET THE HOTTEST NAMES

Get your favorite authors on your favorite reader, long before they're out in print! Ebooks from Samhain go wherever you go, and work with whatever you carry—Palm, PDF, Mobi, and more.

WWW.SAMHAINPUBLISHING.COM